MW00783505

Pretty Marys all in a Row

Broken Eye Books is an independent press, here to bring you the odd, strange, and offbeat side of speculative fiction. Our stories tend to blend genres, highlighting the weird and blurring its boundaries with horror, sci-fi, and fantasy.

Support weird. Support indie.

brokeneyebooks.com

twitter.com/brokeneyebooks
facebook.com/brokeneyebooks

Pretty Marys all in a Row

GWENDOLYN KISTE

PRETTY MARYS ALL IN A ROW
by GWENDOLYN KISTE
Published by
Broken Eye Books
www.brokeneyebooks.com

All rights reserved.
Copyright © 2017 Broken Eye Books and Gwendolyn Kiste
Cover illustration by gawki; cover design by Jeremy Zerfoss
Interior design and editing by Scott Gable and C. Dombrowski

ISBN-10: 1-940372-31-3
ISBN-13: 978-1-940372-31-0

All characters and events in this book are fictional.
Any resemblance to persons living or dead is coincidental.

pretty marys all in a row

gwendolyn kiste

chapter one

THE TWO COLLEGE KIDS SCREAM, AND THE SOUND FILLS MY EARS LIKE sweet music.

The melody ricochets off the slick leather interior, and the baby-faced driver gapes at the rearview mirror, gapes at me, the ghost in their midst. His gaze anywhere but the road, he looks ready to twist the wheel and thrust us straight into the nearest tree. Personally, I wouldn't care if we did crash—it would certainly break up the monotony of the evening—but it's liable to make a terrible mess for these two. Twisted metal and twisted bones. Ugly stuff.

Fortunately for them, he only quivers and keeps screaming and presses harder on the gas pedal as if that will be enough to outrun me, as if I'm not a passenger too. In the shadows of the backseat, his goateed pal crawls against the door and claws at the lock, his eyes covered with one hand, mouth drooping open, a deep and bottomless well. He wanted a make-out session, but I guess I've never kissed quite the way the boys like.

The air glints with their screams, a gray smoke only I can see. Smiling, I part my lips and quaff their fear like fine wine.

And I was worried tonight would be boring. Haunting is an imperfect science, after all, and this pair of stragglers was the best I could do—clueless fools out for a weekend joyride in daddy's borrowed Lexus. But they're better than I expected, the tune of their terror brimming with the elegance of Glenn Miller, the wink-and-nudge charm of Frank Sinatra, the indelible class of Bobby Darin. They taste of bygone summer evenings and peach cake with a dollop of whipped cream on top, so sweet it makes my teeth ache.

"Thank you," I say and turn toward the darkness. I don't need them to stop the car, which is good since they're still screaming and wouldn't hear my request even if I hollered it. To escape, I simply close my eyes, and the sharp crack of night whips around me. When I look again, the hapless boys are gone, their car vanished around the bend, and I'm alone.

The highway, my forever companion, is a trimming of black satin before me, and I stand perfectly still at the center of it, the soles of my heels resting on the solid yellow lines. I should go home now. I've gotten what I came for. But I'm still restless.

And I'm still hungry.

The constellations wink above me, and I start walking. There are no houses here, only a narrow shoulder and a ribbon of potholed asphalt no one's bothered to repair in twenty years.

Overhead, the spruce trees huddle together, and sap drips from the cusps of the branches like fresh tears. It must be spring now, though I can't be sure. Ghosts have no way of telling time, no tally marks etched in the woodwork to track our days. There are no appointments to keep except to be here on this highway to meet the darkness when it calls. And that could happen any night of any season.

I hesitate and tip my head back to the sky. A cab of so-called men, buzzed with whiskey and soda, is coming my way. My mouth waters, and each of my fingers curves into talons. Even from a quarter mile off, they blister through my blood. They'll be such easy pickings. The best are the ones who never see it coming. And why would they see it coming? Here I am, smiling in the gloom, arrayed in satin and pearls as fancy as a daydream at midnight. It's a flawless disguise.

The pickup truck rounds the bend, and I nearly levitate off the ground with excitement.

"Hey, baby," sing-songs one of them, a greasy fellow half-hanging out the backseat window. "How much?"

Too much, I want to reply, but their wolf whistles and deep-throated cackles would drown out anything I have to say. They aren't what I hoped for. Up close, they taste of ash and iron, so I turn away and let them pass. And I don't look back. There's no point. What's behind is gone, and what's gone is as good as dead.

Not that anything, even the past, is as dead as me.

Still, it's a pity they didn't stop. Those drunken dupes long for an unforgettable night, and that's exactly what I can offer. Of course, I could catch up with them if I liked. I drift back toward them, ready to materialize in the bed of their truck—that would really get them, me taking over what's theirs—but behind me, someone else stops. A dinged-up red station wagon with a frill of rust around the bumper. My heart quickens, and I clasp my fingers in front of me, a ladylike flourish, but it's only to keep my hands from shaking.

The passenger door flicks open, and the console light illuminates a familiar face.

"Hi, Rhee." David smiles at me. "Need a ride?"

Always, I think, but I say nothing. He shouldn't be here. He should be at home, away from ghosts and lonely highways, and I should wait on the road for a more suitable driver, someone I'll be eager to terrorize.

I gulp down a heavy breath, ready to tell him to go. But David smiles again, and I know it's hopeless to argue.

Hands still quivering, I slide inside the passenger seat. It's not slick leather like the college boys' car. The upholstery is stained and worn as an old burlap sack. A sea of matchbooks decorates the interior, the small, folded covers in neon and pastel and bold colors, the stench of sulfur lingering lightly on the air. I laugh to myself. David doesn't even smoke and never has, but he collects these souvenirs everywhere he goes, which isn't many places. A seedy bar at the county line or an old Italian restaurant downtown. Any nostalgic locale that still believes in smoking jackets and smoke-filled rooms and femme fatales always in need of a light.

As I settle in for the ride, the matchbooks should crinkle beneath me, but I weigh less than air, so the detritus never notices I'm here.

But David notices. With a steady hand, he reaches over me and closes the door.

"Where to?" he asks, but he already knows. We've got three miles ahead of us. No more. No less.

The highway smears past the windows, briars and weeping trees and abandoned storage sheds all meaningless inkblots in the night.

David's fingers curl around the wheel, and he glances over at me in the darkness.

"It's been a while," he says. I wonder how long a "while" is, but tonight, I'd rather not ask. "How are you and your sisters?"

I hold in a rueful laugh. They're not my sisters, not really, though I don't correct him.

"We're the same as always," I say, not looking at him. "And how are you?"

He hesitates. "All right," he says, but the tremor at the end of his voice tells the truth. That's one thing David and I share: home isn't always where you want to be. I don't know much about his life away from this road, except for the collage of crooked pictures affixed to his dashboard with strips of yellowed tape. He doesn't glance at them much, so neither do I. I try to pretend that there is nothing else. It's just me and him and the highway.

We've taken this path together a thousand times. Every trip is different.

Some evenings, he tells me jokes, silly wordplay that makes me laugh.

Some evenings, he describes the waking world beyond here. It almost makes me grateful I'm dead.

Some evenings, we say nothing. We sit back and retread the same stretch of road, listening to the whir of the asphalt beneath us as if it's the sweetest lullaby.

Some evenings, he doesn't come at all. And that's okay. I'm not always here either. He doesn't know when I'll appear, and I don't know when he will. That makes nights like this even better.

The rusted spires of the fence emerge in the distance, and my throat tightens with disappointment. That metal border is as far as I can go. Tonight's ride is over. It never lasts as long I hope.

David guides the car to the shoulder, and the engine cuts out. I gaze at the sign that hangs over us.

Resurrection Cemetery.

They say this is my final resting place. I'm not so sure. I've paced up and down the green manicured rows a hundred times, around crooked obelisks and between crumbling mausoleums. I've never found a tombstone that looks like mine. Not that I remember my own name anymore, but I'm confident if I saw it again, I'd recognize it like an old friend.

In the meantime, Resurrection Mary is as good as any other moniker. At least, it's got a pleasing rhythm to it. Of course, it's not as pleasing as Rhee, but not everybody knows my nickname. I wouldn't even want them to.

From far away, my home pulls at me, drawing me back to where I belong—not the highway and not the grave but somewhere claustrophobic and confining and worse. I steady my hands in my lap and do my best to ignore the gentle call of my sisters. I'm not ready. I haven't even taken my evening stroll through the cemetery yet. David exits the car and comes around to my door to open it. I don't need his assistance—I can slip through anything at will—but he's always doing his best imitation of a gentleman. And with my candy-sweet smiles and tailored satin, I'm doing my best imitation of a lady.

Outside, the moonlight blurs his face, and for a moment, he looks the same as the night we met, back when he was an eighteen-year-old out hot-rodding for the weekend and I was the same ghost looking for a ride.

"You okay?" He tips up his chin, and the years return. The shadows reveal the deep grooves around his eyes and the sunspots speckling his cheeks. Peaks and valleys, the topography of a life. He ages, but I do not, and we both envy the other for it.

I step out of the car, and he reaches for my hand, but his fingers slip clean through me. This should be no surprise to either of us, but we're fools to the marrow. There's always an instant we both believe this time will be different. This time, he'll reach out, and I'll be there, whole and real, not a ghost but a girl, as common as dust. And together, we'll leave this place behind for good and all.

But I never change, and somehow, our shared sliver of hope makes it all so much worse.

He smiles at me, a beaten expression that twists like barb wire in my chest. I can't bear any of this, the charade of it all. Before I can stop myself, I ask the one question I should keep to myself.

"How's your wife?"

His face goes gray, and he steps back as if I spit fire at him.

"She's fine," he says at last.

"And your daughter?" I glance at the dashboard and the pocketsize photograph taped haphazardly to the space closest to the steering wheel, closest to his heart. There she is with that cherubic face, all ruddy cheeks and sprightly cowlicks. She looks like his wife. She looks a little like me too.

"Abby's well," he says.

The breeze turns cold, and we linger together at the edge of the cemetery fence. Remorse blossoms in my belly like cancer. I shouldn't have asked. This would have been a nice night if I hadn't asked. But sometimes, speaking it aloud is the only way we remember what's true. My feet heavy as granite, I pace through the gates of the cemetery. David follows. Out in the late-night nip of spring, we wander in silence between the headstones.

The tug of my home becomes an all-out pull, and I know that I can't resist it much longer. I want a choice in where I go—and when—but that's not how this works.

David must recognize the look on my face, the defeat drifting behind my eyes, because he shoves his hands in his pockets as if to say goodbye.

"Great to see you, Rhee," he says. "It's always great to see you."

I inhale and taste the air between us, as potent and bitter as heartbreak. "You too," I say.

With his head down, David shuffles back to the car. I wait until the engine rumbles to life and he disappears around the corner. Then I close my eyes. All alone, my body rises up and collapses in on itself like the paper folds of an origami lotus.

The concrete and cemetery fall away, and I dissolve, a sugar cube in hot tea. For an instant, I'm trapped between the highway and home, the here and there, in a darkness that's all encompassing—I'm completely lost, completely gone, even less than the ghost I usually am.

I should be afraid of this part, but instead, I float in the ether, nearly slumbering in my calm. This is the only moment I ever feel truly alone. Or truly safe. There's nothing here, which means there's nothing to hurt me. I wonder if this is what death feels like. It must be nice to rest, to never worry about haunting or family or boys that grow old while you stay young. It must be nice for nothing to matter.

But tonight, not even the darkness offers comfort. My breath catches, and I realize I shouldn't have given thanks for being alone. Because for once, I'm not. Something draws closer to me, a hazy outline that's almost iridescent in the shadows. It twists and gleams, and its presence is cold, even colder than the dead—and that's something I'm an expert in. I can't see a face, but a voice boils like blood in my ears.

Pretty Mary. Pretty, pretty Mary.

Every muscle in my body returns to me, no longer dissolved into nothing. I'm liquid and free-flowing, flying and falling all in the same moment. My lips struggle to form the syllables for *hello* or *who are you* or *what do you want*, but no sound comes out. I'm voiceless and empty and paralyzed in the presence of this invader.

I want to scream, but I don't have time. As effortlessly as it descended, the voice is gone, evaporating like summer rain on concrete, and I'm alone on the steps of a house I wish I didn't recognize.

Welcome home, back to my very own prison.

chapter two

THE WORLD WHIRLS AROUND ME, AND I COVER MY FACE WITH BOTH hands to block it out. It always takes a moment for the nausea of travel to dissipate.

"Normal motion sickness," my sisters say, as if anything about us qualifies as normal.

But I don't need to glimpse the sagging facade in front of me to know what it looks like. I could shut my eyes forever and still see this place. It's seared into the backs of my eyelids. A dilapidated house on a lonely lane in the middle of nowhere. I'm standing on the back stoop, the trim around the windows the shade of old urine, the faded stonework as dejected as first love.

Except on our evening journeys, we can't leave this place. It's our sanctuary and our cage, wrapped into one.

I hesitate and listen again for the voice, but it's retreated back to whatever sovereignty it calls home. Or maybe it was never there at all. Maybe what I heard was only the echo of the wind. Nature can be quite the trickster. An inadequate lie to tell myself, but it's the best I can do.

My hands unsteady, I move toward the door, but the hinges creak open first.

"You're late." From the other side, a sentient tangle of greenery emerges in the doorway. Beneath thick vines of poison ivy, two eyes glare out at me.

I smile back. "Good evening, Mistress Mary."

Even after all these years, she's a fearsome sight to behold. Bloodroot and foxglove and wolf's bane billow to the floor like a chiffon debutante gown. Thorns are peppered all over her body, the perfect accents to complete the ensemble. Everything about her is poisoned and dangerous. In this house, we are nothing if not treacherous.

"Dinner's almost ready." A bloom of wisteria parts, and she thrusts a bundle of fancy silverware at me. "It's your turn to set the table."

A ludicrous request. At meals, we don't ever use utensils. We don't need them. Our dinnertime chores, as proscribed by Mistress, are useless rituals. But then most of our rituals are useless. We still breathe, though our lungs take in no air. Our bodies are skilled at make-believe, carrying out the sacraments of lives we lost long ago. It aches inside me how close we are to existing yet how agonizingly far away.

Mistress pokes my arm with a fork. "Hurry now," she says, but I linger unmoving in her shadow. I should tell her no. I should remain on the back step and never stir from this spot. She can call for me, and she can plead, and she can ring the dinner bell we don't even have, but I'll stay here. And anyhow, I'm not even hungry.

"Rhee?" Her voice softens like butter in a skillet. "Please?"

I sigh and cross the threshold. There's never any point in arguing with Mistress Mary. In our house, she's the oldest—or we think she is. Since we can't remember our lives before, everything is guesses and approximations and maybe-this but probably-not-that. She certainly acts like the oldest.

I take the knives and forks in my fisted hand and trudge into the dining room to set the table.

"Hurry now," Mistress calls after me before retreating to the kitchen. But I'm not rid of her. A tendril of poison ivy breaks away from the vegetation and slithers after me as if I can't be trusted with my chores.

"I'm going," I protest, but it follows at my feet all the same.

In the dining room, I'm not alone. Mack is already arranging a stone goblet at each place setting. Her fingers are raw with splinters, and she smells of earth and rusted nails and funeral bouquets of wilted carnations. She's been toiling away in the basement again. She probably got home early tonight just to get to work. Every evening for more than a lifetime, she's been busy building the same thing: a coffin. Her own coffin.

I position a pair of forks and a knife for myself, her rhyme ringing on repeat in my head.

Mary Mack-Mack-Mack.
All dressed in black-black-black,
With silver buttons-buttons-buttons
All down her back-back-back.

Mourning garb. That's the only outfit Mack wears. Appropriate enough in this house, I suppose. She hunches over the table, and the curled posture makes her look even smaller than she is. Though we have no way to know for sure, she looks like the youngest in the family, her cheeks flushed and dewy and still chubby with youth. If this is the way they put her in a coffin for real, she was no older than sixteen when she died. A child. A baby, even.

I stalk around the table, arranging silverware, still humming her tune aloud. I don't know who taught me the nursery rhyme—sometimes, I think these nothing songs are embedded in us from birth, the melodies stitched into our blood.

As I sing, Mack doesn't glance up. Maybe she doesn't remember her own tune anymore. She shuffles to the sideboard and adjusts a row of hurricane lamps. We have no matches in the house, but that doesn't matter. The oil never runs low, and we never have to light them. They burn all night for us.

"Mistress is angry with you," Mack whispers.

I place a knife at the head of the table. "So?"

"So you shouldn't stay out so late." She straightens each of the chairs, her nervous hands always searching for something to occupy them. "It's not fair to the rest of us."

Not fair. As though any of this is fair.

"Who cares if I'm ten minutes past curfew?" I stop and glare at her. "We have an eternity, don't we?"

Mack shrugs, her eyes downcast and gray. Instantly, my stomach clenches with shame. She's only trying to keep the peace. In this house, we need somebody who tries. My lips part, ready to apologize, but the tendril at my feet has other plans. As if to chastise me, it coils around my ankles, and I trip across the antique rug.

"Knock it off," I say, and the vine hisses at me through green teeth before scurrying back toward the hall.

I grip a butter knife between my fingers, clenched knuckle-white, and my body nearly leaves the floor as I imagine pouncing on that vine and using the blade to sever it in two. Afterward, I'd prod and play with the two verdant halves, watching them wriggle like a useless, dying worm in the afternoon sun. (The sun—I miss it almost as much as I miss being alive.)

But the vine's too quick for me. It slithers into the shadows and flips open the swinging double doors of the kitchen, returning safely to Mistress's side. Sighing, I turn back to the table and console myself that butter knives are far too dull to bisect a vine anyhow.

Besides, dinnertime is about to commence. In the hallway, the stairs lurch, and the rest of the family is here to join us.

Mack smiles. "We're in here, Lew," she calls, in a childish sing-song.

"Coming, darling!" With her long cape billowing behind her, Lew strides in through the doorway, her gait jaunty, hips swinging in time to the creaks of the house. Under one arm, she carries a horse skull. We don't know where the cranium came from or if the horse died of natural causes, and since Lew certainly isn't telling, we've decided it best not to ask.

And that's not the only thing Lew carries tonight. A burnished antique mirror the color of stardust dangles from her clenched hands. Inside the reflection, Bloody Mary drips crimson and waves at me.

"Hey, Red," I say, grinning.

"Evening, Rhee." A drop of blood trickles through the glass and plops on the carpet.

"Don't bother to greet me or anything." Lew shoves Red into my arms. The mirror quivers in my grasp, and I try too late to smile at Lew, but she's already sashayed off to the corner to sulk.

"Don't worry," Red whispers. "It's not your fault. She's in a wicked mood tonight."

It's easy to guess why. By the look of her wan face, Lew found no easy marks this evening. We've all been there. Haunting is no sure thing. Some evenings, in our travels, we come up roses and thorns and nightmares. Some evenings, we come up with nothing.

But that won't keep Lew down. To cheer herself up, she kneels at her secret-not-so-secret liquor cabinet and pulls out a bottle of Viking mead. Like her skull, we don't know where the booze comes from, but on our worst days, none of us complains about the bottomless stockpile of liquor.

"Are we ready?" Mistress glides in from the kitchen with a stack of plates, her vines and poisoned petals twisting and hissing and whispering at us. I shake my head. *Mistress Mary, Quite Contrary. How does your garden grow?* Not with silver bells and cockle shells, that's for sure. More like barbs and venom and insults.

We hustle to the table, and I set the mirror in the chair next to mine.

"Thanks, Rhee," Red says, smiling.

Across from us, Lew sets her goblet aside and fills her skull with mead.

Mistress taps her file-sharp fingers on her placemat. "What have I said, Lew? No skulls at the table."

The muscles across my back stiffen, and we all brace for what comes next.

Lew leans forward, grinning. "If you dislike skulls so much," she says, "then perhaps we should lob off your head and bury it in the garden. After all, we wouldn't want it too close to the table."

Jaws set, they glare at each other across the baroque finery and wish the other one dead. They're already decades too late to get what they want.

I sigh. This is the same as it always goes. Mistress won't be disobeyed, and Lew won't conform. It's a fight that never ends. It doesn't help that, though she rarely says it, Lew resents us.

"Everybody's heard of the four of you," she mutters anytime she's imbibed one too many skull's worth of ambrosia. "But how about me? Nobody knows some wassailing girl with a horse skull."

Sometimes we argue with her—"I'm nobody, the same as you," Mack comforts her—but no matter what we say, we know it's true: Mari Lwyd isn't exactly a household name. The legend doesn't even include her, per se. It claims she's just a hobby horse with a skull fastened to the top. What an indignity. But then not every ghost gets to be a superstar. Better luck next time, Lew.

When the glowering peaks in an inevitable stalemate, Mistress and Lew scoff and look away from one another. I shake my head because this is us, our complete family, as much as we're a family at all. We're a house brimming with Marys, the mortar bursting at the seams with urban legends and deranged nursery rhymes. We don't know how we got here, and we don't know how to leave.

But for now, fleeing doesn't preoccupy our thoughts. All that matters tonight is dinner. With a proud grin, Mistress regards the mirror. "Would you like to start, dear?"

Red smiles. "Certainly."

She can't reach through the reflection, but the fear has no trouble escaping. Red holds up her hands, and blood oozes out of her fingertips. It seeps through the mirror and out the bottom, drip-drip-dripping from the silver trim like a leaky faucet. We extend our goblets, and Lew guzzles the rest of her mead before holding up her horse skull. The fear pools in our glasses, and together, we sip the sweet nectar. The fear is honeyed and familiar like cotton candy melting in our mouths—cloying but oddly satisfying.

"Divine," Mistress says, her eyes half-closed.

I lick a drop off the edge of my glass and sneak a glance at Red. "The twins again?"

Her cheeks pinken. "Naturally."

She's told me about them. They're her regulars—a pair of high school sophomores from somewhere outside of Kalamazoo who can't get enough scares.

"They call to me nearly every night," Red says, flashing me an impish grin anytime she talks about them. The daughters of traveling professors, the girls live alone among piles of their parents' withered textbooks and their own wild imaginations. It was one of those books that taught them how to conjure Bloody Mary, how to do it in a way that she'll always appear. After midnight, they dim the lights and ignite enough candles to burn down the whole house. Then they dress up in their grandmothers' antique weddings gowns ("Just to look extra creepy," Red assures me), and after reciting some obscure verses peppered with Latin, they chant her name three times in their bathroom mirror, squealing with terror and delight each time she shows up.

Red smiles. "Sometimes I think they do it because they're as lonely as we are."

"I wish I could meet them," I say. I wish I could meet anyone other than the lonely passengers on the same stretch of highway. But that's not the way this works. There's no mixing for us. When we hunt, Red's in the mirror, and I'm on the road. Mistress wanders through gardens, and Mack's confined to the dark of funeral homes, her half-finished coffin strapped to her back. Lew has the most mobility, roaming from door to door like a caroler, but even she tends toward the same rundown neighborhoods in the same forgotten cities. This is the way it's always been, though we don't know why.

With the twins' fear buzzing in our bellies, Mistress sits back in her chair, contentment curling on her lips. "And Rhee? What do you have for us this evening?"

I fidget in my chair. I know why she's looking at me. Lew wasn't the only one who struck out tonight. From their pallid complexions, it's clear that Mistress and Mack have nothing to share with us either. If not for Red and me, the whole family would go hungry.

I hesitate before holding out my hands. Smoke curls from my palms, and together, we inhale. I taste tonight all over again, the music and the forgotten summers and the peach cake with whipped cream, and I taste something else. Ragweed and vinegar and the pale underside of a shrunken orange peel.

Lew recoils from me. "David, right? You saw David tonight?" Her nose curls up at his name, as if he's sour milk in a teacup.

There is a long, aching silence at the table, and though the rest of them aren't as bold as Lew, they're thinking the same thing: he's a distraction. He's trouble. Boys are always trouble. Anybody who isn't one of us is trouble.

At once, the evening is over. Spoiled by David. Spoiled by me. Without a word, Mistress folds her napkin into quarters and stands from the table, and we clear away the knick-knacks from dinner. The decorative silverware is shoved back into drawers. The plates and goblets and even Lew's skull are rinsed and polished. The tablecloth is tossed aside, and a fresh one is smoothed into place. These are the same chores every night. We've performed them a thousand times before and will probably perform them a thousand times more.

And now comes the waiting. Morning is almost here, so we return to our places in the house, the places only we belong.

Mistress slips out the back door and wanders in her garden, plucking thorns from rose stems and sucking the blood that blossoms on her fingers.

Lew lingers on the front porch, crooning strange carols that sometimes make me want to scream and sometimes make me want to weep.

Mack creeps down the stairs to the basement and works on her coffin that will never be finished.

Red can go nowhere on her own. She's at others' mercy, only venturing to where she's called or carried. Tonight, I'm the one to oblige her. With a gentle hand, I pick up the mirror and tow it to the master bedroom.

As we crest the stairs, she gazes out at me, her face close to mine but never touching, like two kids colluding at a slumber party.

"I wish it wasn't time already," she says, her wispy voice more air than words.

"I wish that too," I whisper, and we tiptoe inside the bedroom. My hands trembling, I hang her on the wall next to the drooping four-poster bed. She looks at home there, the mirror handsome and secure in the shadows. I give her a half-smile, but my lips twitch at the corners. Things shouldn't be this way. No one should be so alone, not even ghosts.

"It could be worse, Rhee," Red says. "We're sort of together. All in the same house anyhow."

What she means is, *At least we have each other.*

"Miss Bloody Mary," I say and prop my hands on my hips in mock dismay, "don't you go getting sentimental on me."

Her eyes blink twice, blink blood, and she smiles. "Never," she says, a drop of red oozing out the bottom of the mirror and onto my hand.

Smiling, I touch the reflection to say goodbye. I tell myself this farewell won't last, but time moves differently for the dead. Sometimes I fear I'll never see her again. And more than anyone, she's my family. I've never had a sister, not one I remember anyhow, but Red is as good as a sibling. Probably better.

"See you soon," I say before moving for the door and closing it behind me. At last, it's my turn to lock myself in a cage.

On the third floor, my jail is the largest in the house. It even boasts a chandelier. Decadent, no? But I suppose a chandelier is practically required in a ballroom. And with its vaulted ceilings and marble archways, that's what it is: a once-glittering ballroom, now past its prime. Grime lives on everything here—the chandelier, the stained-glass windows, the art deco wallpaper. But despite the sheen of gray, this place always ripples with a cold familiarity. Each night when I tiptoe through the double doors, I can feel the past budding up beneath my skin, and I stand quietly, hopeful that it will break through, that it will come to me. A memory of who I was.

They say I died walking home after a dance. This floor must be fashioned after that ballroom, the final place I visited before my long ride into eternity. It's certainly expansive enough to host a barrage of horny young people whose feet itch for a good two-step. If you ask me, people don't dance enough anymore. So many of the world's problems could be solved with a good waltz or salsa.

The lights dim overhead, and I sway in the soft embrace of shadows. The air heaves with the lonely scents all old houses share: dust and mold and misbegotten dreams. Our home is more misbegotten than most.

But I won't think about that now. I'll just listen to the music that doesn't exist. "Moonlight Serenade." Glenn Miller seems to be the order of the day. Glenn Miller should always be the order of the day.

Somewhere, I hear it playing, distant but unmistakable, the static of the speakers crackling and the gentle purr of the phonograph turning on. My throat buzzes with the melody as I hum it out of tune, my tired body twisting in lopsided circles, my pirouettes ghastly enough to convince me that I wasn't a prima ballerina in my past life. One occupation struck from an endless list of possibilities.

The last scraps of the evening dwindle away as I dance, but morning might as well be a myth in this place. We know only night. I haven't seen the sun since I came here. Sometimes I wonder if I've ever seen it. But I must have because otherwise I wouldn't know what it was. I wouldn't remember the butter-yellow rays spilling across the horizon, or the sweet warmth sinking into me, past the bone and right down to my soul. That means even if it's lost to me now, there was a before, there was a version of me who wasn't this exiled beast, feasting on pain. This gives me hope. Out there somewhere, could there be something better than this?

My eyes flutter. Tomorrow is gathering closer. Something else is closer too. That discordant voice returns, scraping against my skin like claws.

Why don't you dance with me, pretty Mary?

My breath catches like a stone in my chest, and I seize up. Nestled elsewhere in their gilded cages, can the others hear these words too? Or is this voice for me alone?

"Who are you?" I ask, but once again, the sound fades away like a faraway echo. Only this time, it's replaced with something else.

A distant weeping like a choir of a thousand girls mourning as one.

At first, I think it's coming from within the house, but these aren't my sisters. The five of us don't cry, maybe *can't* cry. These are the sobs of strangers.

I want to stay awake. I want to keep listening to the shadows. But I'm no match for the dawn. The moment the sun rises, my eyes close, and a shroud of darkness embraces me, as intimate and cruel as a lover.

Then I too fade away.

chapter three

I OPEN MY EYES, AND IT'S NIGHT AGAIN. SWEET STARS THE COLOR OF SUGAR crystals are strung overhead, and I'm on the highway, my satin gown pressed and my pearl necklace polished. There is no hint of last night on me. No trace of our shared meal or stain from Red's blood or sheen of dust and regret from the ballroom. Tonight, I'm fresh and new. And worst of all, I'm hungry.

But maybe the hunger is a good thing. If the last few dinners have been any indication, Mistress, Mack, and Lew will be returning home empty-handed and wan as ever.

Fortunately, the highway is generous tonight. The moon has barely risen before I'm offered a ride. And it's a charming one. A whole Volkswagen van of wannabe hippies, ten of them total, each arrayed in tie dyes and buckskin, their gaunt bodies stuffed between and behind and under the seats, filling every available space. And as it usually goes with hippies—those original to the 1960s or these modern-day ones—all of them are way too trusting. They smile and pull over and squeeze me in, though it doesn't take long for them to realize their mistake.

I do my best vanishing trick, blinking in and out, the veins under my skin turning phosphorescent, and I must be a fierce sight because soon there isn't a calm soul in sight. Their eyes bulge before closing up tight with tears, and their fingers are stuffed inside their gaping mouths. But even that doesn't stop their screams.

Their fear isn't sweet like Glenn Miller. These hippies holler and sob in time to Bob Dylan, his early stuff from his Greenwich Village days. Not my usual style, but they're plenty satisfying. In the crammed backseat between the dangling bead curtains, the biggest challenge is telling the difference between the plumes of their fear and the residual pot smoke. I quaff more than my share of both.

Head humming, I slip through the van and back onto the road. Their screams hang in the air around me, and I smile as they speed off into the night. Not only did I dine well this evening, but my free-wheeling meal tickets will now have a most charming ghost story to pass down through the patchouli-soaked generations.

"Attend all the best activist rallies for peace and love," they'll tell their progeny at bedtime, "or else the evil Mary will get you."

This makes me grin wider, the thought of my name being evoked for the sake of social causes. I don't know why the other Marys are coming up short on scares. There are certainly enough unsuspecting victims on the highway. Surely, in the gardens and funeral homes and far-flung neighborhoods, Mistress, Mack, and Lew can find someone to haunt.

My belly fizzling and full, I skip along the highway, giggling like an excitable schoolgirl, my heels dipping in and out of potholes, until headlights flash against my skin. David's dinged-up station wagon coasts to the shoulder. I don't wait for the door to open before I slide inside.

He nods at me, his face more lined than usual. "Where to?" he asks.

"Anywhere you want," I say and wish it could be true.

We drive for a while, the tires singing an elegy beneath us. David grips the wheel with one hand and clasps a small yellow matchbook with the other. I gaze at the faded logo on the paperboard: an old motel on Route 1 that's probably been out of business for a decade. His eyes still on the road, David plucks out a match and scrapes it against the book to light it before drawing it to his lips and blowing it out again. The air in the car blooms with the loneliness of sulfur and smoke. Sometimes I think he only collects matchbooks to keep himself occupied, his fingers always fiddling with them when he's nervous.

I lace my hands together and wonder what's bothering him tonight. After all, it's a perfect evening, crisp and lovely and cold. Too cold. The last time I was here, it was the debut of spring, but now it feels later in the year.

I hesitate, gnawing my bottom lip. "How long has it been?"

David gives me half a smile. "Not long," he says and does his best to sound cheerful about it. "Only three months."

My breath heaves in my throat, and the contact buzz from those hippies melts away. It's been a quarter of a year since yesterday. Three months that feels like a single night. Time for me is malleable and cruel, and I hate it, how life slips away like grains of sand in an open palm. I blink, and it's gone.

Sometimes it's one month. Sometimes it's three. Sometimes it's more. And I never know for sure until I come back and ask David.

And that's only if David is around. Once, I had returned to this highway, and he wasn't here. I passed dozens of nights without him, my chest twisting tighter each evening.

When he finally showed up one Sunday night an hour before dawn, I thought the worst was over—all the wondering, the what ifs. The car edged to the shoulder like always, and I smiled at him through the smudged window, but his ashen expression didn't change.

We drove in silence for a while. That was the first time I saw a photo taped to the dashboard. There was only one then—a pocket-sized glossy featuring him stone-faced in a tux and a girl in a white veil that looked like me.

"I didn't think you were coming back," he said as though he was obligated to explain. He wasn't. I would never expect that from him. I only had one question.

"How long?" I asked, not looking at him.

"Long enough," he said. "Too long."

Five years. It had been five years since we'd seen each other. For months, he'd returned to the highway, but I never appeared, and eventually, he resigned himself that I wasn't coming back.

"I'm only here tonight," he said, "on a whim."

He told me he'd been married six months, and he smiled a little when he confided about his daughter, already curled up and dozing in his wife's belly.

"Congratulations," I said and meant it. He deserved it. One of us should have a life. That was only fair. And it's not like he and I could be together. No courthouse is eager to issue a marriage license to the dearly departed.

I never cried about it. Ghosts don't cry. But that night at the dinner table, the smoke poured from my hands in long, chartreuse tendrils.

"Exotic flavors," my sisters said, and that was when I learned what sorrow tasted like.

David leans back in the driver's seat, his brow damp and heavy. "I've missed you," he whispers.

I wish I could say the same. I wish I'd had enough time to miss him. But this only feels like tomorrow. It's only a moment to me.

The sedan halts at the cemetery gates, and we take our usual path, past the headstones with names etched deep in granite. Being here is always the same. It feels like walking in circles but worse. It's walking nowhere at all.

I kneel before a tombstone and trace the letters with my fingertips, pretending I can feel the grooves, cold and deep beneath my hands. How strange that the most permanent part of most people's lives are the monikers they leave behind in stone after it's too late to matter.

"I almost remember it, you know."

David looks at me. "Remember what?"

"What it felt like to be alive. To see morning come." My hands clench into fists so tight my fingers ache. "Sometimes the almost-remembering is so much worse than the not-remembering."

The moon dips in the sky, and my home tugs at me. But I'm not ready yet. I don't want to return to the darkness, to the place where the voice discovered me yesterday.

I want to stay here, I think. Without looking at me, David nods.

"So do I," he says, answering words I never spoke.

I move close to him, and his breath fogs straight through me.

"David," I say and clasp my hands in front of me to keep myself from shivering. "Could you do something for me?"

He searches my face, the hopefulness in his eyes almost too much to bear. This is something I've never done. Before now, I've never asked him for anything.

"Name it," he says.

I hesitate. I always promised I would make no requests of him. It seems silly to me, how the living become indentured to the dead, doing their bidding, fulfilling their unfinished business. I've never wanted to shackle him to me. But this request is a small one.

"Could you bring something? A book maybe or an old newspaper article? Something about this cemetery or the highway . . . or me."

I'm asking him to find a ghost story for a ghost.

"Rhee," he says, and my name sounds all wrong on his lips. "I'll try, but it's not easy. People aren't sure that you're even . . ."

I stare at him, dread burning in my guts. "That I'm what?"

"Real." His cheeks redden, embarrassed that he accused me of not existing. All the bright hopefulness behind his eyes is gone. "But I'll try."

I smile. "Thank you."

From far away, my family beckons me.

"See you soon," I say to David and hope it's true.

As I drift toward home, falling between here and there, my body weak and watery, I strain against the darkness. I don't want to hear the voice from yesterday, coaxing me with its worthless words, and I don't want to meet its face as it floats toward mine. But as I spark and fold onto myself, I see nothing, hear nothing. No voice croons in my ear, and nothing dances in the gloom around me. For an instant, I think I'm lucky. I think I'm alone.

But a flash of something formless twists around me, and I can't move or think or scream. The thing in the darkness isn't drawing nearer. It's already here with me. I know because I can hear it breathing, faint and hot and wet against the back of my neck. And its arms don't need to emerge before my eyes because they're already around my waist, looped in a ring, not quite touching my skin but near enough to embrace me if it wanted. And perhaps that's the point: to show me that it can take whatever it wants.

I'm still waiting for that dance, the voice says, but I don't reply, my tongue shapeless and numb in my mouth.

When I'm deposited back on the front step of the house, I'm breathless and nauseous and turned inside out, but I have no time to gather myself together. The horizon is pink with dawn, and Mistress is already waiting on the porch.

"You're late," she says, and her vine slithers toward me and wraps itself loosely around my ankles. "You're really late this time. We have no time for dinner now."

"I'm sorry." I stumble into the house behind her. "I didn't mean to."

For once, this is the truth. I never used to be able to stay so long with David.

At the table, Red and I offer the sustenance we gathered from the evening. Lew, Mack, and Mistress have nothing to share. They won't look at us when we ask why not. They say nothing in the dining room, but afterward, as I grasp the mirror and head toward the master bedroom with Red, the three of them conspire in the corner.

"Go ahead," Mistress says when I hesitate on the stairs. "Get tucked in for the morning."

My heart in my throat, I trudge up the winding steps with Red in my arms. Behind us, the other Marys whisper their barbed secrets. Something is wrong, and they won't tell us what. Dust and fear crawl down my throat, and I choke on the musty air.

In the bedroom, I hang the mirror on the wall, but unlike most evenings, I don't skulk away to my prison. The voice will be there again in the ballroom, my unlikely partner as I dance to music no one else can hear. And I won't run to it. I'll stand here, firm and stubborn against the night. If the darkness wants me, I'll make it wait.

"Rhee?" Red presses her hands into the glass. With blood dripping down her body like brackish water, she resembles a harpooned mermaid peering through a porthole. "What's wrong?"

"What do you think they were saying downstairs?"

She laughs. "Are you worried they were talking about you?"

"No," I say. I'm worried they're talking about something else. Something worse. Something that would explain why the voice is speaking to me and why Red and I are the only ones with successful haunts.

Red shakes her head. "How bad can it be? I mean, the worst must be over. We're already ghosts." She grins at me, and I smile back at her. She won't let me be upset. If I start to look too glum, she'll joke or keen banshee-sweet or drag her fingernails across the underside of her own reflection until her own ears bleed.

"What does a ghost need blood for, anyhow?" I used to tease her, and she would ooze red out of her eye sockets just to spite me. I was the first one to call her Red. We all have nicknames now. Five Marys in one house are bad enough, but five Marys without nicknames are downright confusing.

But these days, we don't feel like five Marys anymore. We barely feel like anything at all.

"I asked David to bring me something," I say. "A book. About us. About me."

Red hesitates. "Do you think it will help?"

I shrug. "It can't hurt."

She runs her hands through her hair, thick with blood, and a narrow river of red seeps down the glass. "The twins have found a dozen books about me. About the Bloody Mary folklore and its origin. It never tells me what I hope to learn." She laughs. "And none of the illustrations ever look like me either."

I shake my head. "Maybe what David finds will be different."

"Maybe." Red smiles again, and I reach out to say goodbye, the way I always do. Only this time, the glass between us ripples at my touch.

I jump back, the muscles across my shoulders tight with surprise.

Red gapes at me. "What was that?"

I breathe in, and the air that fills my lungs is light and sweet as dew. "I have no idea."

I touch the mirror. It's solid again.

"Rhee," Red whispers. "What's happening to us?"

I only wish I knew.

David arrives early on the highway. I don't ask him how long it's been. The snow coating the trees like powdered sugar tells me it's been longer than I'd like.

He brings me a crumbling book, an encyclopedia of oddities, and opens it to a two-page entry on Resurrection Mary.

"This is the best one I've found," he says as we nestle in the frozen grass, close but never touching.

I run my fingertips over the black-and-white face of a girl, dour and wide-eyed and no older than twenty. This is supposedly me, the dearly departed all the scholarly folklorists claim I am.

"We don't even look alike," I say and think of what Red said last night about the illustrations of her.

David plucks a piece of grass between his thumb and forefinger, avoiding my gaze. He knew I'd be disappointed. As though it's his fault nobody knows more about a ghost.

I keep reading. "They aren't even sure what happened to her," I say and catch myself. "What happened to *me*. This says I died in 1934. Or 1927. Or maybe another year altogether."

David shrugs. "That's the way it works, I guess," he says. "With ghosts, I mean. The details are always sketchy. People can't narrow it down. In the appendix, though, it says that there have apparently always been hitchhiking ghosts."

I chirp out a tiny laugh. "Is that what they call me? A hitchhiker?" I curl my legs into my chest, envisioning myself as a Dust Bowl waif, bindle on my shoulder, thumb stuck out to the wind.

David's face flushes as though he's the one with the reason to be embarrassed. He doesn't stand accused of vagrancy.

Because my hands are worthless here, I stare at this same page for an eternity. "Where did you get this book?" I ask, desperate to fill the empty space between us.

"From home," he says.

I laugh again. "I mean before that."

He hesitates. "The librarian at my high school. She gave it to me at the end of my senior year. Said I'd get more use out of it than her."

I watch him. "You've had this book that long?"

He looks down at his hands, fiddling with nothing. "After you and I met, I had to tell *someone*," he says, his voice snapping apart. "I figured she'd call me crazy. Instead, she tried to help me figure out who you were."

Tried to help. Never succeeded.

I gaze closer at what is supposed to be my picture. It seems strange not to recognize your own face. In the pixilated image, a haphazard scan of a faded snapshot, there's a small scar the size of a keyhole over her eyebrow.

"She was in a fire." I lean closer to the picture. "That's where she got that scar."

David peers over my shoulder. "Where does it mention that?"

"It doesn't," I say. "I remember her telling me."

"Telling you?"

I swallow hard and nod. This isn't me. But I know her. Somehow, I know her. I can't remember anything about myself, but I can remember that.

"I have a couple other books," David says. "I'll bring them next time. They aren't as good, but maybe they'll help."

"Help me do what?" I ask, the defeat sinking like a quarry stone in my chest. "Be dead?"

He stares at me, his eyes dark and wounded. "To be wherever you want to be," he says, and the defeat inside me dissolves, replaced with sour dread. I know what he's thinking. He wants me to be free, so we can be together. Driving in his crummy station wagon, sitting at home at his dinner table with his daughter and maybe his wife. He forgets I'll still be me. A ghost, lighter than air and just as useless.

I'm suddenly on my feet and running through the graveyard, past the obelisks, away from David and his daydreams. It aches inside me, imagining us together. I close my eyes to escape this moment, but in the darkness, something is already waiting for me.

Pretty Mary. Why are you leaving? Don't you know I'll always catch you?

Shadows dance behind my eyelids and coalesce into a shape, all dark angles and hideous points. I try to back away, try to open my eyes, but I can't escape.

A hand. In the gloom, a hand is reaching toward me.

You belong to me. All you pretty Marys belong to me.

The fingers twist toward me, and I'm caught in its grasp. I gag up bile and fear as its cold touch sears through me, down into the bones I once had.

I wrench away, the might of my own fury forcing me back, and I topple toward the earth. Because I'm not solid, there's nothing to stop my fall, so my body slips halfway into the dirt before I catch myself.

David calls my name and rushes to me.

"I'm fine," I say and struggle to pull myself free. On instinct, David reaches for me, but his hands slip clean through me. As always. The curse we somehow forget.

I crawl out on my own, my hands grasping at nothing as I pull myself from the impromptu grave. When I'm on my feet again, I see it. A welt in the shape of five curved daggers around my wrist. Right where the darkness touched me.

David stares at my arm. "Rhee?" His voice is thin and scared.

My dry lips purse, but I can't speak. All I can manage is to rub my wrist, as though the blemish is a stain, not a wound.

"David," I whisper, but it's too late. It's nearly dawn, and the pull of my sisters is too much for me. I drift backward, folding in on myself, smaller and smaller until I'm nothing at all.

At the dinner table, I have nothing to share. I was too busy with David to haunt. Other than Red's offering from the twins, we go hungry. To fill the vacant timeslot, Mistress argues with Lew over her skull, and the rest of us hold our breath.

"Put it away until later," Mistress keeps repeating.

Lew rolls her eyes. "I know you like to pretend," she says, "but you're not really our mother. You're not our sister. You're nothing. We're all nothing. You know that, right?"

"Don't," Mack whispers. "Don't be cruel."

Lew's head snaps toward her, and what's left of the evening collapses around us. Everybody except me is screaming. Even Red gets in on the action, hollering through the glass about us getting along and how we have no reason to complain.

"At least you're not trapped in your own reflection," she half-growls at us.

The room shifts and contorts and turns inside out. The table levitates off the floor, and the silverware dances on our placemats like restless bones in the Paris catacombs. Everything is becoming unstable here, and we're letting it. We're letting the thing from the darkness control us.

I press my hands to my face to hold in a furious laugh. My palms smell musky. David's cologne. He can't touch me, but in spite of himself, he's left part of him behind with me. This has never happened before. I've never been able to carry him with me. I curl my fingers tight and clutch his scent to my chest.

"What's happening to us?" I whisper. "And what's so hard about scaring? You've been doing it for years."

"Not anymore we can't." Mack's eyes are as gray as dust, and she won't look at me. "They can't see us anymore."

The whole world holds still for a heavy, aching moment.

I stare at her, digesting her words. "What do you mean?"

Lew grunts. "She means, we're dying."

"But you can't die," I say. "You're already dead."

"We're fading then." Mack fumbles with a silver button that's come undone from her jacket. "We're disappearing."

I move toward her and grasp her hands in mine. "You're here," I say, pressing her skin into mine. "I can feel you."

"That's great, Rhee." She wrenches herself free. "But you're the only one. Everybody out there can walk right through us and never notice."

"Like we're not even there," Mistress says, and the vine twitches limply at her feet.

They say nothing else. There is, I suppose, nothing else to say. They just excuse themselves from the table and retire to their prisons.

But I won't depart so quietly. Upstairs in the master bedroom, I sit cross-legged on the floor in front of the mirror, my palms clasped together as if in prayer. But prayer would be hopeless. Even if I believed in something, I wouldn't know who to pray to. And I don't think anybody answers ghosts anyhow. If they did, we probably wouldn't be ghosts in the first place.

Red rests her forehead on the glass. "What are we going to do?" she asks. "You and I can't bring enough to the table for all of us. They won't last like that."

She's right. Even if we wanted to, we can't survive without dinner. We've tried. Twenty years ago now, back when David was young—and in a way, so were we—we went on a hunger strike. None of us scared a soul for a fortnight.

This was the first choice we ever made, and we made it together.

"Nobody owns us," Lew had said, and we all agreed, the five of us gathered around the dinner table, hands clasped to hands and mirror. It should have been good. It should have been freeing.

It was agony instead. Our bodies decayed around us, bones jutting out from every angle, skin melting in clumps on the dining room floor. Our eyes turned liquid in our skulls, and our hair shed in clumps. What an overwrought display we were, and I might have even laughed to myself if my skin hadn't been so busy peeling from my bones in strips of tanned leather. Plus, it's hard to speak, let alone giggle, when your tongue withers to cinders in your mouth.

But no matter which of our parts disintegrated next, we never faded out like last spring's daisies in December. We simply went on existing—the best we could. As it turns out, there are things in this world so much worse than death.

When we finally returned to haunting, it didn't take much for us to terrify people. Our bodies gaunt and gnarled, the grotesquerie was too much for even the strongest stomachs. David tried not to grimace when he saw me, and his expression is one I still can't forget. And he wasn't the only one. A regular of Lew's—a little blue-haired lady on the outskirts of Des Moines—even suffered a seizure and was hospitalized for a week.

We've never gone hungry again. It's safer for everyone that way.

"What if people are forgetting us?" Red asks. "What if that's why they're fading away? What if all of us will fade away?"

"That won't happen," I say. "It *can't* happen."

She stares at me, her gaze thistly velvet against my skin. "How do you know?"

"I don't," I say. "But we'll figure something out. We'll get out of this."

The dawn comes too soon, and once again, I'm on the highway. My entire body quivering, I bring my hands to my face. David's scent is gone. I should expect nothing else, but the disappointment still bubbles up in my chest.

I start walking, start scaring, start the cycle all over again. And like the best nights, the moon dips, and David's station wagon coasts to the shoulder. I smile to myself. This is what I need. To see him and to read the books he promised to bring me. I'll find a way out. We'll find a way together.

I move toward the passenger's side, but I don't get in. That's because tonight he's brought someone else with him.

"Hi," a tiny voice chirps.

His daughter sits in a gray booster seat, wearing pigtails and a smile.

"My name's Abby," she says brightly. "And I already know who you are."

I edge away from the car. "I'm fine," I say. "I don't need a ride tonight."

I whirl around—away from David, away from the car, away from that little cherub in the backseat. She can't be real. Other than that picture on the dashboard, she can't really exist. And I can't be close to her, not with the darkness courting me. I shouldn't even be close to David, but he doesn't care. He throws the car into park and flicks open the driver's door.

"Rhee, please." He chases after me. "Don't go."

I turn back and gape at him. "What are you doing?"

"I'm visiting you," he says, his face drawn, "like I always do."

"This is not like always." I point back at the car. "Why is *she* with you?"

She. I won't even say her name. It's like a curse of sorts, a magic spell that will undo me if the word crosses my lips.

David shrugs as if he too is genuinely confused about it. "I just thought you should meet," he says. "She's been asking about you."

About me. About a ghost. I almost laugh aloud. He's told his daughter ghost stories. I'm a ghost story.

If my fists wouldn't go clean through him, I'd strike him in the chest.

"Why would you tell your daughter about me?"

He swallows hard. "She wanted to know where I go at night. It seemed wrong to lie to her."

I glare at him. "And what do you tell your wife?"

"She never asks."

I hesitate in the chilled night air, staring at him and at the car. I should keep walking. I should run. But I want to see those books. I *need* those books. If I'm going to help my sisters, I have to figure out who I am, who we all are.

My head down, I trudge back to the car with David behind me. On the floor of the passenger's side, a book on folklore is already flipped open to the pages about Resurrection Mary. I slip inside and gaze down at another picture of a girl who's supposed to be me. It's a different girl, this one a few years older than the last, but she still doesn't look like me.

The engine roars, and I focus on the text. I need to memorize this. I need to figure out who we are. Besides, I tell myself this is a normal night. Just ignore the pint-sized beast in the backseat, and everything will be fine.

But apparently, pint-sized beasts aren't eager to be ignored.

"When I grow up," Abby says, her legs bobbing up and down in the booster seat, "I want to be just like you, Aunt Rhee."

I dry-heave and bring up a mouthful of smoke. "No, sweetie," I say and twist around to look at her. "You don't want that. I promise."

"Sure, I do." She smiles at me with her crooked milk teeth. "Daddy says there's nobody as incredible as you."

David chokes on air, his fingers bone-white around the wheel. "I never said . . . *that*."

"Yes, you did, Daddy." Abby beams as if this is a delightful game, and only she remembers the rules. "You said, 'Aunt Rhee is an incredible person. I hope you can meet her someday.' You said that, Daddy."

I double-over in my seat, and remember the girl from the last book David brought. I close my eyes and see her face somewhere dark and lonesome, and I see something else. A flash of faded gingham like a quilted comforter or maybe a curtain. And a broken picture window, the crack in a shape of a spider web.

"What's wrong, Aunt Rhee?" Abby asks.

Everything, I want to say. This is all wrong. If I'm not this girl in the picture, who am I? Am I anyone at all?

Yes, I'm someone who wishes she wasn't here. I wish I was out of this car and away from this little girl and the flashes of memories I'd rather not have. I should slip through the door and return to the highway. I should keep my eyes closed and just go home.

Or I could make a choice. I could go somewhere else. I could prove to the shadows that we don't belong to them.

"Away," I say. "Far away."

I open my eyes, and the air shimmers black around us. But this isn't the darkness seeping into me. This is something I'm conjuring all my own.

"Rhee?" David's voice trembles. "What's happening?"

He stares at me, and he's gone, vanished before me.

But no, I'm the one who's gone, siphoned from the car and sent somewhere else. Somewhere small and cramped and strange.

A space with a window. On the other side of it, two girls in wilted wedding dresses gape at me.

"Who are you?" they ask in tandem, and I step back from them into a puddle of liquid. Of blood.

"Rhee," a familiar voice, sweeter than the darkness, says. "How?"

My breath heaves in my chest as I see her. Bright and clear and near me for the first time.

Red. I'm standing right next to her.

And I'm inside the mirror.

chapter four

"RED." THE TWINS CREEP CLOSER TO THE MIRROR. "WHY DIDN'T YOU tell us there were two of you?"

"Because there aren't two." Red stares at me, and I can't tell if she's shocked I'm here or indignant I'm encroaching on her space. "Rhee isn't the same as me."

"This is her? This is Rhee?" The twins' faces brighten, and their thin fingers graze the opposite side of the mirror in disbelief. "You're Resurrection Mary?"

"I guess," I say, fidgeting and aware of how inadequate my knowledge is about everything, even myself. With the mountains of books behind them, the twins probably know more about me than I do.

They watch me, their eyes eager, and Red inches closer, as though she isn't sure I'm real.

"How?" she asks.

I shrug. "I don't know."

But that's a lie. I'm here because I asked for this. I wanted to escape David and Abby, to flee that moment in the car. I wanted to make a choice. And that's what I did. But now that I got what I asked for, I'm not sure what to do next.

But Red knows. Her fingers quivering, she takes my hand. For the first time, I'm holding my sister's hand.

Then it's gone. I lose the focus that brought me here, and my fingers slip through her palm. She screams my name, but I can't scream back, the words clogged like glue in my throat. Red reaches for me, her hands grazing my wrist, my shoulder, my throat. She grasps at my necklace, and for a moment, it's the only thing that tethers us together. But it's too weak to bind us for long. The clasp snaps against the nape of my neck, and one by one, the pearls cascade to the floor. Red falls away from me, the twins fall away, and I'm tipped backward in darkness.

Alone in the darkness.

I blot out the world with both hands, my body tumbling through nothing. I expect the voice to find me here, but it's entirely, unnervingly quiet. Everything is quiet. The thing that lives in the shadows must not have expected this. I didn't expect it either.

When I open my eyes, the world still swirling, I'm back in the station wagon. It's parked in front of the cemetery. This is ordinary, so painfully ordinary, that I wonder for a moment if I never left, my trip to the mirror no more than a wishful fever dream. Then I reach up, my fingers quaking, and touch my collarbone. The pearl necklace is gone. I left it behind with Red.

This is real. I escaped this place. I finally made a choice of my own.

Slumped over the steering wheel, David gapes at me, his face gray and laced with sweat. His lips mouth something—a prayer maybe, or a question—but the words dissolve before breaching the air.

Abby, however, isn't like her father. She's not afraid of the ghost that blinks in and out of existence. In the backseat, she giggles and claps her hands.

"Neat trick, Aunt Rhee. Can you do it again?" She leans forward in her booster seat, eyes wide and flashing. "And can you take me with you?"

I return home early. Tonight, the highway was no place for me to linger. David wanted to know what happened, and while I couldn't blame him, I couldn't explain it to him either. I can't even explain it to myself.

"I'll see you tomorrow," I said, though we both knew it could be a week, a month, or a lifetime until we meet again.

"Bye, Aunt Rhee!" Abby waved brightly. "See you soon!"

Mack is already in the basement, toiling away at her coffin. The pounding of the hammer trembles through the house like an irregular heartbeat, and I shudder at the sound. Lew and Mistress aren't back yet, so I creep upstairs. In the master bedroom, the mirror is on the wall where I left it last night. And Red is already inside, home early just like me.

"We need to tell them," she says. "About what happened."

She's right. And it's not the only thing I need to share. I still haven't confessed to anyone about what I've seen and heard in the shadows. I nearly laugh aloud to myself. And what will I say? I don't even know what the voice is. And what if it's not there at all? What if I'm just crazy?

I steady my hands in front of me and wish that I was merely crazy. That would make this all so much better.

We're halfway through dinner—Red's offering from the twins as our appetizer, main course, and dessert—before I can gather the courage to speak.

"Something happened tonight," I say, and the words are so silly and inadequate that I want to scream.

But it's enough to get my sisters' attention. Their eyes flick up at me, and my entire body goes numb. They won't believe what I say, and I don't blame them. But I have to tell them. I take a deep breath for courage, and I hold it in until my chest aches. Then I blurt out, "I went into the mirror."

"With Red?" Lew's face scrunches up. "You went into Red's mirror?"

I nod, and the world shrinks in from all sides like a corset yanked tight around my waist.

"That's ridiculous." Mistress tidies up her place setting, posture straight as a steel rod. "That's not how this works, Rhee, and you know it."

"But it's true." Red holds up my necklace as proof. I smile. In the time since I visited her tonight, she's gathered up all my stray pearls and restrung them on the wire, good and gleaming as the day I bought them. A day I can't even remember.

"A trick." Lew rolls her skull beneath her open palm. "We're fading out of existence, and the two of you are playing tricks."

"It's no trick," I say.

"But it must be," Mack says, her arms folded across her belly, cradling her hunger like a swaddled infant. "You know we can't reach each other. That's against the rules."

"Whose rules?" I say. "And even if there are rules, maybe they're changing. Maybe what happened to us is somehow tied to what's happening to you."

Lew wheezes out a shrill laugh. "So you two get to socialize while we slowly starve to death." The skull quivers beneath her fingers. "Sure, that seems fair."

"Maybe this can help us," Red says, a drop of blood like a teardrop in the corner of her eye. "*All* of us."

"I don't see why we're talking madness." Mistress shoves back her chair and glares at me. "If you want to talk about magic tricks, Rhee, then prove it. Walk into the mirror right now."

My throat closes up, and I hesitate, all gazes on me.

"I don't think it works that way," I say.

But to be fair, I'm not sure. I have no idea how it works.

"It's like I thought." Mistress circles the table toward me. "You can't do it."

Looming over me, she reaches for my hand—to slap my wrist like I'm a wayward child or maybe just to tether herself to me, her kin—but whatever she wants, it doesn't matter. She can't hold on. Her entire arm becomes translucent as water. Tonight's meal was far from enough to keep her with us. As though in retaliation, as if it's my fault, the vine swats at me, but it slips right through my ankle.

None of us moves. As quickly as it happened, Mistress is solid again. She hasn't left us for good, not yet, but she will soon. All three of them will. We're almost out of time.

"I won't listen to this tonight," Mistress says. "I won't listen to any of it."

She rushes outside to her garden without another word, and at once, dinner is over.

"Way to perk up a meal, Rhee," Lew says with a scoff before heading for the front porch, somewhere far from me.

Mack is the last to leave the table. Still clutching her gnawing hunger, she sighs and trudges toward the basement.

At the door, she turns back. "I wish it were true," she says and disappears down the steps.

My heart heavy, I embrace Red, the only one who believes me. Outside, Lew passes by the window and reclines on the porch swing. I listen for a moment as she creaks softly back and forth, but no elegiac melodies curl sweetly from her lips. Everything in the house is quiet and haunted.

I take Red upstairs and hang her on the wall.

"Are you okay, Rhee?" she asks.

I hesitate. "Something else happened today," I say. "I remembered something. A place."

She peers out at me, her face pressed against the glass. "The dancehall where you were that night?"

I shake my head. "It was a house, I think. But run-down. Everything there was faded and broken."

Not the home I thought I'd find.

Red watches me. "That's a start," she whispers. "We'll figure this out."

I nod, though I can't imagine a way that she could be right.

In the ballroom, I pace along the walls, the distant tunes of Duke Ellington as this evening's accompaniment. But there's no comfort here tonight. My family is fading, *will* fade completely unless I can fix this.

I close my eyes and strain to return to the place I found today. The place from my memories.

And I see it again. Cracks in the window. Gingham on the walls. And something else. Engines whir overhead. They rumble into my blood, and I think how others are traveling—but not me. I'm still. I'm alone.

Never alone, pretty Mary.

I open my eyes, and the shadow curls around me.

My fingers clench into tight fists. "You know what's happening to Mack and Lew and Mistress," I say, half-choking on my fury. "You're the one responsible, aren't you?"

Not exactly. But rules are rules. I just enforce them.

"So my sisters are disappearing." The truth is ash in my mouth. "What about me? And Red?"

The shape in the shadow laughs, and the sound rakes against my ears like talons. *All in good time, pretty Mary.*

"You can't have me." Rage burns deep in my chest, and I move toward the darkness. "You can't have any of us."

You won't get a choice. The shadow drips down from the ceiling, stretching like saltwater taffy, and it wraps around my throat. Duke Ellington fades away, and his smooth voice is replaced with another sound.

Weeping. Far away, girls are weeping again.

"Not tonight." I grit my teeth and stare into the roiling shadows. I stare until my eyes blur and focus again, focus into something deeper. Something that makes even the darkness uncomfortable.

Your time is almost here, pretty Mary. Like it or not.

The darkness dissolves, and I'm alone. Whatever comes next, I already know I won't like it. And I also know I won't wait here for it like a fool.

Though I've never once tried it, I leave the ballroom before dawn. Nothing holds me here except tradition. And it's time to shatter that ritual like a wicked looking glass.

I march down the stairs and slip out the back door. Mistress lingers in the center of her garden, her chin tipped to the earth, as though meditating. The manicured rows of her sanctuary, once verdant and dangerous, have retreated to a sullen brown. Everything here is dying.

I rustle through the overgrowth, and she glances up. For a moment, she looks at me like I'm a stranger.

"Rhee," she says as if reminding herself.

"I'm sorry about tonight." I circle her, the vine at her feet too listless to pursue me. "But I wasn't lying. Something did happen."

"I believe you, Rhee," she whispers. "I just think it's too late to matter."

"It's not too late," I say and hold her hands in mine. "We don't have to wait for the end to come."

She nods and wraps her fingers tighter around mine. "If you can do this—"

"If *we* can do it."

The sun crests over the horizon. Tomorrow is almost here. We're running out of time.

"Tonight, you come to us," Mistress says, the dawn flickering like wildfire in her gaze. "Or bring us to you."

I smile and close my eyes.

I look again, and I'm back on the highway. David is already waiting there.

And so is someone else.

The passenger door of the station wagon is wide open, and Abby sits on the seat that's usually mine. "Hi, Aunt Rhee," she says, waving.

I wave back at her, my body steel against the night. "Why did you bring her again?" I whisper to David.

He kicks the dirt. "Because she asked."

I scoff. "And do you always let a four-year-old tell you what to do?"

His gaze locks on me. "You mean, when I'm not letting a ghost tell me what to do?"

At this, I scowl but don't answer. It's a trick question anyhow, so I ask something else. "How long have I been gone?"

David shakes his head.

My stomach twists. "That long?"

"No," he says. "Not at all. It's only tomorrow."

I exhale, and my breath fogs around me like smoke and fear. That's good. That's what I wanted. To reach him before it's too late.

"I thought I lost you last night," he says. "When you vanished from the car. I thought that was it, that you were gone."

"I know." I hesitate. "Something's happening to us, to my sisters. And to me."

He nods but says nothing.

"I need to try something. I don't know how it will turn out." I stare hard at him. "Will you stay with me?"

He looks at me, his face gaunt with shadows. "Always."

I don't know if this will work, but I told Mistress that I would try. More than ever, I wish that I could take David's hand, that I could hold on to something real and ground myself to this place. But I can't, so with my eyes squeezed closed, I focus. In the darkness, a darkness that doesn't belong to the voice in the shadows, my sisters' faces materialize, and I pull them toward me. First, I bring Mack into sharp focus. Sweet, little Mack. Our baby sister.

I open my eyes, and the highway's still here. I don't feel any different.

But I'm wrong. Something is different. At my side, Mary Mack is staring at me, her coffin slung over her shoulders like a too-heavy bookbag.

"Rhee?" she asks, her voice thin and warbling.

I take her shaking hand in mine. "Stay with me," I say.

But I'm not done yet.

Lew. Next, I imagine Lew. And then I see her, standing in front of me. But not on the highway. She lingers on a doorstep, crooning a beautiful dirge no one can hear.

Like Mack, she stares at me. Unlike Mack, it's more a glare. "What are you doing?" she asks, more annoyed than impressed.

With my free hand, I entwine her fingers with mine. "Mistress," I say. "We need to pick her up next."

And with that, we're in a garden somewhere. Not the garden in our backyard, but a real orchard. My body is numb from boomeranging back and forth. This is imperfect and uncomfortable, like a kid peddling unevenly on her first bicycle. But it's working.

"Good evening, Rhee," she says and loops her arm through Lew's.

We're together, the four of us. But it's too much, and I can't hold on. My focus dissolves, and I topple backward through the gloom to somewhere else.

Nausea grips my body, and the world returns to me, one piece at a time.

Cicadas in the trees. A rush of bald tires on concrete. A chill in the air.

The highway. I'm back on the highway.

But I'm not the only one. Though I couldn't grasp them tight, it doesn't matter. The four of us are here, side by side at the gates of the cemetery.

David stares at me. "What happened?"

"My sisters," I say breathlessly, pointing next to me. "I've brought my sisters."

He searches the air helplessly, twisting all the way around like a drunken fool. He shakes his head. "I'm sorry, Rhee," he says. "I can't see anyone."

The car door still open, Abby giggles from the passenger's seat. "Daddy, of course, you can see them." She holds out her chubby little fingers and counts us off. "One, two, three, four. Four pretty ghosts."

She nods once, a kind of self-congratulations, and I'm not sure if she's proud of herself for spotting ghosts or for counting that high. Either task is as ordinary as dirt to Abby.

I hesitate. "These are my sisters," I say, because introducing ectoplasm seems like the polite thing to do under the circumstances. "This is Lew and Mack and Mistress."

They each wave at Abby, and she waves back.

"Nice to meet you," Abby chirps.

Lew looks from her to me and back again. "She can see us? That little girl can see us?"

That little girl. The perfect mark. My muscles turn to stone, and I heave in a breath.

"Lew, don't you dare—" I start to say, but I'm too late.

Lew lunges forward, a masquerade already in motion. It's been so long since someone could see her that she's pulling out all the stops. Her skin drips down her bones, revealing the sinew and organs and marrow beneath, transforming into her most frightful self—all to terrify Abby.

I try to cut her off before she reaches the car, but Lew's faster than me. She's everywhere like a shadow draped over the world. At the sight of what Lew's become, Abby exhales tiny curlicues of smoke, red as a dangerous sunset, but she doesn't scream. Not one yip. Instead, her arms flail with wild abandon, and she squeals with glee. Even once Lew backs away, face returned to her, Abby won't stop grinning.

"Do it again, Lew," she says, her cheeks flushed. "Scare me again."

We all inhale the smoke—me included shamefully—and Lew smiles. "I can do that, little one." She moves forward, her face swirling and changing, but I shove her back with one finger.

"That's enough," I say, and with a glower, Lew flips her hair and turns toward a rusted spire of the cemetery fence. She already got what she wanted anyhow.

David watches me and watches Abby and watches the air between us before gaping at me. "Rhee?" His voice wavers. "What's going on?"

I wish I could explain it to him.

I wish I could explain it to myself.

Dinner that evening is a grand affair.

"We must have our best tablecloth!" Her complexion bright, Mistress hurries about the dining room with the vine at her feet as impetuous as ever. It trips me three times before I've even set down all the silverware.

Red shakes her head. "And you, leaving me out of all the fun," she says.

"I didn't mean to," I say. Tonight was over so quickly I didn't have a chance to pick up Red. "I'm not sure how it all works yet."

Red grins. "I'm only teasing," she says. "It's good you got them out."

But what if I can't get you *out?* I want to ask. So far, I've only gone to Red. I haven't brought her to me. What if there's a reason for that?

But it's a question that has to wait until after dinner. Although we only have Abby's fear to dine on—and of course, another generous helping from the twins—it's plenty to satiate us.

We sit back at the table, and for an instant, everything seems calm and kind and okay. Like we're a circle of friends or even a real family, good and whole.

Like we aren't ghosts.

"I don't want to ruin dinner," Mack says. "But what now?"

We all look at her, unsure how to respond.

She sniffles and traces her finger along the woodgrain of the table. "Because other than some little girl who's mostly impervious to fear, no one else can see us."

Lew shrugs. "Maybe Abby will be enough."

"No," I say, my chest aching. "We can't rely on Abby. She's only a child."

"Don't blame me." Lew cracks her back, and a shiver like a spider runs across my flesh. "You're the one who took us to her."

"We went there together," Mistress says, her voice resolute, and she's right. It's not just because of me. The four of us went as one. We chose to stay together. We're changing the rules. Whatever's in the darkness, we can beat it.

We're stronger together.

A warmth flushes through me. Maybe that's the key. If we're together as a family like we are here every night, maybe we could do anything.

"They can't see you in their world," I say.

Lew laughs. "Yeah, Rhee, we already know that."

"So then," I say, smiling, "we bring them here."

chapter five

"**B**UT WE DON'T HAVE ENOUGH TIME TO PREPARE THE HOUSE."

This is Mistress's primary complaint. Her only complaint, in fact, or the only one she voices aloud anyhow. But even this protest is without any weight because Lew, Mack, and I are already up and out of our chairs, readying the house and readying ourselves, deciding how to make the house its most formidable self—"more cobwebs and bones obviously," Lew says—and deciding that whatever we do, it must be done tomorrow night.

"The sooner, the better," Mack says.

More like, the sooner, the less likely we evaporate into nothing.

"So"—Lew yanks cobwebs from behind the sideboard and her liquor cabinet and drapes them like streamers from the ceiling—"who do we invite?"

Invite. That word sounds so polite, the notion of issuing invitations rather than simply stealing someone from their world and pulling them into ours.

"I'm sure the twins would be interested," Red says. She sits inside the mirror, watching the rest of us work.

Lucky Red, not having to lend a gory hand.

Unlucky Red, suspended alone in her glass coffin.

"I have someone in mind too," Lew says, smirking to herself.

"How about you, Rhee?" Mistress swathes our longest, reddest runner over the table. It looks like the whole dining room is bleeding. "Are you inviting anyone?"

By anyone, she means David. They all wait, their heavy gazes lingering on me, needling me for a response. My chest tightens. I want to say no. I want to keep him out of this, especially until I'm sure I can do it correctly. What if something goes wrong? I don't want him in the first-round trials.

My sisters are still watching me, so I just shrug.

"If he wants to," I say at last.

Lew grunts. "Of course, he'll want to." She tosses her skull in the air and catches it. Over and over, the head goes up and down like a child on a trampoline. I look away to avoid becoming seasick.

"If we did disappear," Mack says, pausing in the doorway of the hall, "what would happen to the house?"

Silence settles among us, the sixth figure in the room. The house—and how we found it—is something we'd rather forget. That's because when we arrived, it was already furnished like it was expecting us. Like it had already been lived in. We assumed the previous occupants would return, but when no one came calling, we tried to forget. It seemed the safest thing to do under the circumstance.

Mistress breaches the silence by asking each of us what terrors we plan to contribute to the party. "I'll be doing the floral arrangements, of course," she says.

"I'll do the centerpiece," Lew says and lobs her skull into the middle of the table. It lands with a thud, and she nods once, pleased with herself.

Red promises extra blood. "As much as I can bring to the party," she says, no particular inflection in her voice. She has an odd, wan look about her, and when she glances at me, I mouth, *What's wrong?* But she shakes her head and turns back to watch Mistress.

"I have something," Mack says. "For decoration."

Hands clasped in front of her, she scurries to the basement. A moment later, she lugs her coffin upstairs on her back and leans it against the corner of the dining room.

"I think it's finally finished," she says.

"About time." Lew grins at Mack and admires the finished piece.

"This will do very nicely as décor," Mistress says, and her vine curls into the coffin and spruces up the pink satin liner inside. "Well done, Mack."

Mack blushes with pride, and in the hurricane-lamp glow of the dining room, she looks no older than a child.

We finish readying the downstairs, ensuring it's as dusty and creepy as we can make it. Dawn edges dangerously close, so we retire to our respective rooms, each of us giddy as schoolgirls. Each of us except Red.

In the master bedroom, I stare at her. "Are you okay?"

She shakes her head. "Aren't you worried about tomorrow?"

"Of course," I say. "But we can't stay like this. We can't stay here forever."

Blood drips from her fingertips. "What if this is all a cycle? What if we think we're choosing, but this is just part of the game, of what we're supposed to do?"

I'm chilled and tied tight inside, but I won't let her know that. "Then we'll find out tomorrow," I say and place my open palm on the mirror. Through the glass, she matches her hand with mine.

Upstairs, on the marble floor of the ballroom, I whirl in circles. We're so close now. Tomorrow is so close.

The darkness sways at my side. *It's still not too late to dance with me, pretty Mary.*

I put my back to him. Not tonight. I don't want to see him tonight. Not when the shadows play tricks with the light and form into something that looks real. Like a man, broad and hulking and dangerous.

What would you like me to bring to your party tomorrow night?

My stomach clenches. "You're not invited," I say.

You keep telling yourself that, pretty Mary. Either way, I'll see you soon.

At that, he dissipates into the night.

"Goodbye," I say. The darkness can come, but he won't stop us. My sisters won't fade. We'll be together, and we'll become stronger than we've ever been. We'll get out of here. Not even darkness can keep us.

Through the ballroom windows, the dawn pours like honey on my skin, and I fade away.

When I open my eyes, I don't know if it's night or day. And I don't know where I am. This isn't the highway. The room is cramped and gray, and something sticky pastes itself to the bottoms of my heels.

Blood. I'm already inside the mirror.

Red wanders the dark space, spiraling the edges of the room.

I smile and blink away last evening. "Hello again," I say and entwine my fingers with hers. Her skin is cold and smells of roses.

"Hello, Rhee." She squeezes my hand, but her face is pale and strange. I pretend not to notice. This is right. This is the way it's supposed to be. I'm here, and the party is about to begin.

"What do we do now?" I ask her.

She shrugs. "We wait. Hopefully, the twins will call to me."

"They'll call," I say.

But I'm wrong. We wait for what feels like hours, the silence nearly deafening.

"Go ahead," Red says at last. "Gather everyone else. You can come back for me at the end."

I want to argue, I want to stay with her, but we don't have enough time, so I cover my eyes and focus.

Lew. I see Lew. Tenuously, I pull myself toward her, listening for the heartbeat she no longer has.

When I look again, I'm standing next to her in a narrow kitchen. The walls are arrayed in garish green and orange flowers, and the entire place is ripe with jonquil and jasmine and stale air freshener.

"Where are we?" I ask, still queasy from the trip.

"In Des Moines," Lew says.

"Des Moines?" I hesitate. "You mean, at the house of that little old lady you scared half to death?"

Lew stares at me defiantly, as if she was expecting this reaction.

"Yeah, so? I like her. She's *nice*," Lew says, stroking that last word as softly as a beloved tabby. "She's been trying to get me to bake cookies with her for years. She doesn't seem to understand that I can't hold a wooden spoon."

But the old lady doesn't seem particularly nice tonight. All she can do is glare at me and shake her cane in my face.

"You aren't my Lew," she says and braces herself against the stove. "Where is my Lew?"

"She's right here." I motion next to me. It must look like blank air because the old lady grimaces.

"Don't get sassy with me, youngster," she says. "I might not be so spry as you, but I haven't gone soft in the head. Not yet anyway."

Lew rolls her eyes. "I don't know how you're going to convince her to go anywhere with you."

I sigh. "What's her name?"

"Gladys."

"Hello, Gladys." I inch forward, half convinced she might really smack me with that cane. "You can't see her, but I assure you that Lew's here with me."

"Lew? Darling?" Gladys flails wildly at the air. "What did you do with her?"

"Lew will tell you all about it soon. But first, I'd like to take you somewhere. If that's okay with you."

"A trip?" Gladys eyes me up, one fright-white eyebrow curled in suspicion. "Will it be by motor coach?"

I hesitate. "No, at least not the kind of motor coach you're used to."

She purses her lips. "Will meals be included?"

"Again," I say, "not your sort of meals."

Gladys pauses, considering. "Will my Lew be there?"

I perk up. "Yes," I say.

Gladys smiles. "Then let me get my purse."

After a moment, she returns, pocketbook and white gloves in hand, and stands next to me as though she's waiting in line for the bus. I breathe in and close my eyes. I've never done this before, and I'm not even sure it will work. But if I can pull my sisters toward me, maybe I can haul others with us. Maybe. I imagine the space between here and there, and I imagine home. At once, a circle limned in onyx encompasses us, and we're in free fall.

"This better not ache my hip," Gladys hollers as we spiral into darkness and crash-land as one on the back doorstep.

I exhale, and my body is so light I nearly levitate off the earth.

It worked. This really worked.

Mack waits here for us, an eager emissary.

"Wonderful to finally meet you, Gladys," she says. "Lew has told me all about you."

Lew and Mack shepherd Gladys inside, our first guest of the evening, but I don't have time to mingle. I close my eyes and materialize back in the mirror.

Red still sits cross-legged and alone.

"Are the twins here yet?"

She shakes her head. "Go to David," she says. "You can come back for me afterward."

As I snap back to the highway—it's my natural haunting place, so there's no need to focus—I worry David won't be there or that he'll come too late.

But he's already waiting for me. And tonight, he's alone. With my heart in my throat, I tell him about the party, about what we're planning. As Lew predicted—oh-so-snidely—he consents without another thought.

I shake my head. "Are you sure you're okay with this?"

He smiles, and the moonlight drapes over his face, fashioning him again into the young man I met back when we were both the same age. "I finally have a chance to go home with you, and you think I'd say no?"

"And what if something happens?" I ask, the question as heavy as lead pellets in my belly. "What if I can't get you back to Abby?"

"You will," he says. "I trust you, Rhee."

That makes one of us. But tonight is slipping away from us, and I don't have time to force him to reconsider. I envision the circle around us, and we're falling. David calls my name and I call his. I fear we might be torn from each other in the darkness, but before we can scream twice, we're on the back step.

"Wait here," I say breathlessly and return to the mirror.

Red is still alone.

"Don't worry about me," she says. "Go home. Get started."

My muscles seize up, and for an instant, I don't move or speak.

"Not without you," I say. "I won't go back without you."

"Maybe this is best, Rhee." She stares down, refusing to look at me. "Maybe I shouldn't come with you. Or maybe we shouldn't be doing this at all. We're messing with something big here. I'm afraid it will mess back with us."

My throat constricts. What if she's right? I part my lips, ready to confess what I've seen and heard and should have told her before now. About the voice. About the darkness. But I don't have time. All around us, the inside of the mirror shakes.

"Bloody Mary," say two faraway voices.

I look at Red, and she looks back at me.

"Bloody Mary." The twins are closer now.

An invisible weight presses into my chest, and I say Red's name, the name I gave her, the closest thing to a real name she has, but it's too late for me to say any more.

"Bloody Mary." The voices are right on top of us and inside us and everywhere at once.

The twins materialize in the glass, and because we don't have time to do anything else, we tell them about tonight.

"We can't be sure it will even work," Red says. Blood oozes down her fingertips and drips to the floor, the plunk-plunk rhythm as steady as a pulse. "Or if it will be safe for you."

Like David, the twins don't listen to the warning. They just beam and nod their heads. "We wouldn't miss it for the world."

My breath shaky, I gaze into the barrier that estranges us from the twins. I focus, and the mirror turns liquid.

Grinning, the twins reach through and step inside to meet us.

"It's cold in here," they say and shiver.

"Do you want to go back?" Red asks, and they shake their heads. But I want to go back. I already want to rewind, so this whole night never happened. Dread churns inside me, and I feel so weak and disjointed that I'm not sure I can do it again. I'm not sure I can get us home.

But Red knows me well, knows me like a real sister. She looks at me, and sensing my reluctance, she takes my hand. With her steady against me, we focus together. The ribbon of darkness encircles the four of us, and with my eyes squeezed closed, I pull us through the here and there, through something even colder, until we're on the back step.

But this didn't work, not completely. The twins are right next to me. But Red is no longer holding my hand. She's *in* my hands, still inside the mirror that I'm suddenly holding. My fingertips graze the glass. It's solid again.

"It's fine," she says, her dark eyes turning to gloss. "Go inside, and get started. We're running out of time."

A knot ties tight in my throat, and I want to argue, but Lew appears in the doorway and takes the mirror from me. I follow her, and she fastens Red to the wall in the dining room.

David is backed into the corner next to the sideboard, his eyes downcast on something in his hand. A blue matchbook for an Italian restaurant in Indiana. He turns it over and over, plucking out a match, lighting it, and pinching it out again, his hands nervous and occupied. I smile a little and wonder if it's this ghostly house that's making him panicky or the prospect of meeting my family over dinner—*our* dinner.

Maybe this will be okay, I tell myself. Maybe we'll get through the night.

David glances up and smiles back. Like some old-timey gentleman, he bows and steps forward to meet me. With hope packed heavy in my chest, I reach toward him. But we can't touch. And it's so much worse than usual. Instead of his hand slipping through mine, I slip through him. I'm solid and real, and he's the one as thin as a midnight breeze.

"That's so cool," the twins whisper, disappearing their own hands through me and through Lew and Mistress, testing their own bodies. "We're the ghosts here."

My stomach curls. What if they're like us now, all of them dead, because we brought them here? Because *I* brought them here?

This isn't what we wanted. I look to Red in the mirror, and from her dark expression, she's thinking the same thing that I am.

What have we done?

But no one else seems worried. Lew tosses her head back and laughs as Gladys thrashes, spearing her noncorporeal cane through Lew.

"At least now I know what the afterlife feels like," Gladys says. "A preview of coming attractions."

Mistress, however, won't waste time on frivolities. "Thank you all for joining us this evening," she says. "For this special . . . party."

Gladys coos. "I always love me a party," she says, clapping her liver-speckled hands. "Will there be punch and petit fours? The best parties always have punch and petit fours."

Lew grins. "Maybe afterward."

"But for now, we want to give you a very exclusive performance," Mistress says. "Is everyone ready?"

The twins flip their long hair and arrange the veils over their faces. "We're ready," they whisper.

Lew gathers her soon-to-be-dripping face. "You ready, Gladys?"

Gladys nods. "Whenever you are, Lew."

David steps forward and smiles again at me. I want to stop this, but it's too late to back away now. Everyone is here, and there's no way my famished sisters will disappoint our guests.

Hand in hand, the Marys and I unite as one. On the end, I interlace Mack's fingers with my right hand and hold out my other palm to the glass—to Red. Inside the mirror, she presses both hands onto mine, and I wish so badly I could feel her there, that she could be with us.

But she's not here, and this will have to suffice. The room goes gray around us—dim but not entirely dark. We have to ensure our guests see what we do next.

Through cobwebs draped thick and lustrous, the walls tremble and begin to crawl. The venomous flowers Mistress arranged on the table and sideboard bloom in tandem, their petals twisting and growing and becoming sentient.

Blood leaks from the cracks in the ceiling, and an old Glenn Miller tune lilts from a nonexistent Victrola. Every note plays backward, a beautiful yet uncanny melody that creeps into our ears and takes hold of our souls.

And then our bodies, the bodies of the Marys, contort at our own will, dripping and bubbling and boiling. Our bones jut out from one angle, our blood drips from another, the sinews and muscles and little wiggly viscera exposed like the most beautiful Christmas tinsel you've ever seen.

And from the lips of our guests come delighted screams as the smoke rises and mushrooms and swallows us up. Blue tendrils, and green and red, every color drifting and twirling and free-form.

I smile. It's working. This is working. The fear swells toward us, and we release our hands and turn our palms upward to devour it. My eyes water, and I can't see my sisters next to me. I can't see anything, not Red on the wall, not David across from me, not even my own hands, although I know my body is still here because it's filling up with the smoke.

But somehow, this isn't right. The five of us are no longer united. In this moment, we've opened ourselves up, like carving into a vein. We've never been this powerful.

Or this vulnerable.

A laugh blisters in my ears, and with dread choking me, I realize we've miscalculated. Oh god, we miscalculated everything.

"Stop," I say, but my voice dissolves, a soap bubble in the air. No one hears me. I hardly hear myself. I want to scream, but it's too late for that.

The smoke dissipates, not much, just enough to cut a space next to me. There's Mack. Sweet, baby Mack, too willowy and trusting for her own good.

Pretty Mary. For once, the voice isn't speaking to me. *Come to me, pretty one.*

Mack frowns and drifts toward the sound. The others can't see her leave our side. They can't see through the smoke and the shadows like I can. The darkness wants me to witness this. It wants me to see what it's about to do to her.

In the corner, Mack steps toward her coffin, the one she toiled for a lifetime to build with her own hands.

The one that's finished now and ready for an occupant.

I call her name and surge forward, my arms fumbling through the fog. The voice laughs again, a hideous noise like a kettle that won't stop screaming even once the burner is cold. At once, the thick walls of the coffin shiver as though they're flesh, and we're not the ones making them move. Mack instinctively knows this—she understands it too late—and though she turns to run, the coffin is eager for the chase. Mack manages only a single step before the pine rises up and tumbles over her, closing her up inside.

She screams once—the baying of a fawn abandoned in a clearing—and pure electricity quakes through my body, the shocks firing up my spine until I wish I could tear out my own bones and never feel anything again. The smokes clears, and the other Marys and all our guests gape at me and gape at the empty space in the room. Without a word, the party is over.

And Mary Mack is gone.

chapter six

THE HOUSE EXPLODES WITH NOISE AND BEWILDERMENT. MY SISTERS SHIFT one way in the dining room and then another, and our guests follow their lead as if this is an arcane dance and they're trying to learn the correct steps. I stand in the center of it all, the silent eye of a storm. Everything around me is a blur of movement with no purpose or direction. We don't know what to do next because we've never dealt with this before.

We've never lost one of our own.

"Mack!" Lew won't stop screaming, as though Mack took a wrong turn down a hallway and needs someone to guide her back to us again. As though it could be so simple.

Through the picture window, the horizon has turned purple and gold. My throat closes up. Dawn is almost here, and our guests can't stay much longer. We've already pushed this too far. With their bodies as soft as smoke, they're hardly here at all. If they linger into the morning, they might not be guests at our home. They might become permanent residents.

"I need to get them back," I say and move toward the twins who are closest to me, the pair of them colluding in the corner.

Lew catches my arm. "You need to help us find Mack."

She glares into me, blaming me, hating me. This party was all my idea, after all. I grit my teeth and blame myself too.

"Go ahead, Rhee," Red says softly, her reflection in the mirror gauzy and distant. "Get the twins home. David and Gladys too."

But Lew only grips my arm tighter. "You have to help Mack."

"I'll help when I return," I say. "They can't stay, Lew. We don't know what will happen to them."

Or how many days will pass if we keep them until tomorrow night. Abby could be grown by the time I get David back. She could be old and withered or interred in the ground. The thought shudders inside me.

Lew glances up at Gladys who shakes her cane at the ceiling and calls out for Mack.

"Fine," she says and releases me. "But come back. *Right* back."

I move for the twins, and with them at my side, I focus. The house falls away, and we plunge into the darkness and back into the mirror where Red is waiting for us.

"Are you okay?" I ask the twins.

They look down at themselves, at each other, and back at me. "Yup," they chirp.

I fixate on the mirror and turn it liquid. It's ready for them to pass through, but they're not ready for it.

"What can we do?" The twins quiver on the threshold of our world and theirs, and the walls tremble in reply. On the other side of the glass, their ceremonial candles from earlier tonight have burned down to the wicks. "Tell us how to help."

"Don't worry about us," Red says. "Go home. And be safe."

"Besides," I say, "I'm not sure you can help."

I'm not sure any of us can.

But the twins are too stubborn to budge. "Maybe we can find out something."

I shake my head. "I've tried."

"But we haven't," they say. "What do you remember, Rhee? About yourself?"

Though I don't have time for this, I know they won't go until I try.

I sigh and close my eyes. "Engines overhead."

"An airport," they say.

I look at them again, but I see somewhere else, the place I'm from. "Sunrise through a cracked, front window."

"The house faces east."

"Faded gingham," I say. "Faded everything."

They beam as if they've been turned loose on the afterlife.

"This will be enough," they say. "We'll find you something."

Tittering, they climb through the glass, and when they're back in their bedroom, the mirror turns solid again, and their reflections vanish.

I need to vanish too, back to the house for Gladys and David. But first, I kneel down and entwine my fingers with Red's. She stares up at me from the floor, a pale sadness washed across her face. Our hands tethered together, I flash back to the house—our prison. I try to take her with me, to pull her out of the mirror, but when the darkness snakes away and I'm back in the dining room, I'm alone, no Red next to me.

"Go, Rhee," she says behind me. "Get them home."

I turn to the wall. Her visage is still in the reflection. She's trapped. Red is trapped, and I can't help her. The darkness won't let me. He's keeping her there, maybe even keeping her from me. And there's no time to try again. With Gladys at my side, I'm gone, the two of us flashing back to her gaudy kitchen in Des Moines.

"Thank you for the party," Gladys says, waving goodbye with her cane. "And don't worry, dear. You're a capable young lady. You'll find Mack in a jiffy."

I smile at her. If only she were right.

My head stuffed with cotton, I focus again and return home. But this trip is worse than the ones before. It scorches through me, and when my feet feel something solid beneath them, I collapse to the splintered hardwood floor in the dining room. Everything about me is heavy and overstretched, my skin too tight and too flaccid at the same time like I'm wearing the flesh of someone else. All this travel in a single night has left me unbalanced, but that doesn't matter. I have one more trip, and it's the most important. I have to get David back before it's too late.

He waits for me in the hallway. Sometimes it seems that's all he can do—wait patiently for me to return for him. The two of us huddle together, and in an instant, our bodies float backward into nothing, into the here and there. I inhale his scents of myrrh and cardamom.

We return to the highway, as cold and empty and worthless as we left it. Here in the chill of the evening, nothing has changed. But back home, everything is different. Everything is wrong and ruined and all my fault. A profound ache deepens in my chest. I need to get back there. I need to help search for Mack, even though searching will do us no good.

But I can't leave David, not yet, not before I know.

I look at him, my lips struggling to form the question. "Are you okay?"

He shrugs and exhales a strained chuckle. "I'm fine."

But I just keep watching him—as if he's not real, not anymore—and caught beneath my gaze, he understands that his word about feeling fine won't be enough. With a sigh like a stone stuck in his throat, he stretches out one hand toward me.

I don't want to reach back. I don't want to touch him and discover he's not there, that the house did something to him, that *I* did something, even though I never meant to. I tell myself he can't be like us. He can't be a ghost like me.

I hold my breath, and my fingers outstretch to meet his. I slip through him. He's solid, and I'm not—the way it's always been. But not the same. This is the first time I've ever been grateful for it.

My heart still tight in my chest, I half-smile at him.

"I'll see you tomorrow," I say and mean it. I'll be back here on this highway as soon as the sun sets. Whether the darkness likes it or not.

I close my eyes and return to the dining room. Red and I linger along the wall in silence as Mistress and Lew pat down the drapes and pull out the couch cushions and overturn all the chairs. Part of me wonders why they're treating Mack the same as a lost handful of coins or a wayward wedding band, but I'm too exhausted and queasy to ask.

On the floor, something flashes near my feet. A blue something. It's David's matchbook. He must have dropped it when he was here. I kneel next to it and try to pick it up, but my fingers slip through the paper. The matches are like him: spectral and not really here.

I clasp my empty hands in front of me to keep from shaking, and I step back toward Red. She starts to ask if I'm okay, but from deep within the house, we hear something else. Something soft and sad and distant. A gentle sob like a lullaby.

Mack's sob.

Lew wheezes out a wail of her own. "Where are you?" Her voice is thin and strangled. "Mack, where are you?"

Another sob from right above us. Lew charges toward the wall, her gnarled fingernails clawing at the plaster. She makes it halfway to the ceiling before her body topples to the floor, but it doesn't stop her. Back on her feet, she twists in wild circles, dizzy with desperation.

"Tell us where you are," Lew says, her eyes the color of weathered slate, "and we'll find you."

The sound drops out around us, and we freeze. Then that voice—that wicked voice, always dripping with sweet malice—fills my ears.

You can beg all you want, pretty Mary. But Mack can't play hide-and-seek with you tonight.

I'm not the only one he's speaking to this time. All of us can hear him now.

Lew gnashes her teeth and scans every crevice in the room. "Who are you? And what have you done with her?"

The darkness laughs. *Why don't you ask Rhee? She knows all about me.*

Lew turns toward me, her lips curled back from her gums, the look of a feral animal ready to pounce.

"You?" The question twists in my guts. "You know who did this to Mack?"

If I wasn't already dead, Lew would finish the job right now.

"I don't *know* him," I say, the words sticking in my throat, thick and clotted as mud. "But I've . . . heard him."

Mistress steps toward me, and I back against the wall, cornered and small and scared.

"For how long?" she asks.

I gag on air and shrug, and without a word, they intuit the answer: long enough. I've known long enough to know better.

Disgust blossoms in Mistress's cheeks. "And you never told us?"

I turn my face away—from the darkness, from Mistress and Lew, and most of all, from Red, because I can't bear her disappointment too. But it doesn't matter. I can still feel them watching me, saying nothing, their expressions colorless and wounded in ways for which I can never atone.

The darkness laughs again, and the sound thrums through the house and deep into my bones. I close my eyes and will myself far from this place and this moment. The room is warmer now. Dawn is nearly here. I can wait this out. Tomorrow will be better. It has to be better. We'll figure out how to retrieve Mack, and I won't seem so terrible for not telling them about the voice in the shadows sooner.

But for now, they won't let me rest. Lew and Mistress draw closer, desperate to yank the answers out of me like intestines.

"Who is he? What has he told you?" Mistress demands.

"This isn't my fault," I say and wish I could believe it. "I wasn't the one who dragged Mack into the shadows."

"But you knew," Lew says, and her sour breath fills my nostrils. She tastes of death and desperation. "You knew, and you did nothing."

I start to speak, my breath shaky and not my own, but morning rescues me. Light pours into the house, and we're enveloped in its embrace. The others melt away around me, and I could be like them. I could let the day overtake me like I always have. But instead, I open my eyes and focus on the horizon. This moment won't slip away from me like the others before. I'll hold onto this sunrise. For all I know, it might be my last.

I see the sun, a glittering coin in the sky, and its warmth sinks into my skin like rose oil. Morning is here and so am I. The darkness can't stop me from witnessing it this time. This moment is mine.

Then it's gone, and I'm back on the highway.

Parked on the shoulder next to the cemetery, David is already here, and I'm grateful, so grateful, that I'm not alone. I'll figure something out. Some way to rescue Mack. Some way to make this right.

But there will be no right this evening. From across the lawn, I sense it on his face. Something's happened. I seize up next to the car, a dozen paces from him, convinced if I move any closer, he'll turn to ash before my eyes.

"What is it?" I ask.

He hesitates. "I'm not sure," he says and reaches out for the rusted fence.

His hand slips clean through it.

My heart compresses in my chest, but before I say a word, he inhales and tries it again. This time, his fingers clench around the spire, and he's whole.

"I noticed it today when I was driving to work." He grunts, and the sound catches halfway between a laugh and a sob. "Made for an interesting commute."

I stare at him, wanting so badly to scream that I have to bite down on my tongue until it bleeds to stop myself.

"Can you control it?" I ask at last. "When it happens, I mean?"

He shakes his head. "It comes and goes," he says. "Like I'm here and not here at the same time."

This is my fault. I've done this to him. And probably to the twins and Gladys, too. They're trapped like us, but they don't even get to be dead. They're something else. Maybe something worse.

I move toward David, but the tether that connects me to home and to my sisters tugs hard at my chest. I brace against it. It's too soon. They shouldn't be calling to me already. But maybe it's not a bad thing. Maybe they found Mack.

Or maybe the darkness found them.

Everything around me spins, and I'm desperate to just stop, if only for a moment. But I don't get that choice. Home yanks harder now, and I taste the sharp tang of sorrow. Red's and Lew's and Mistress's grief. It's copper in my mouth, pungent as blood.

"I'm sorry," I say to David. "I have to go. But I'll come back. I promise."

If I can. If I even get a choice.

David steps toward me. "Rhee," he whispers, my name soft and honey-sweet on his lips, "what's happening to us?"

"I don't know," I say, and I'm pulled backward and home to my sisters.

The three of them are already in the dining room, Red in her mirror and Mistress at the head of an empty table. In the corner, Lew kneels at her liquor cabinet and guzzles straight from the bottle, no horse skull for a goblet this time.

I rush toward Red, and questions tumble out of me. "How were the twins? Were they okay? Did they say anything? Did we hurt them?"

Meaning, did *I* hurt them?

But Red shakes her head. "I don't know." She won't look at me. "I couldn't go to them, Rhee."

Lew scoffs. "None of us could leave tonight except you."

This has never happened before. They've never been trapped at night. I turn away from them, so they can't see the fear in my eyes. "That's not so terrible, right? It gave you more time to search for Mack."

"No, it didn't." Lew charges me and whirls me around to face her. "We can barely hear her anymore. Her cries are fading, Rhee. She's fading, and we can't find her."

But that doesn't mean we're alone. Red gazes through the curtains. "Someone's outside," she whispers.

We hesitate, and a figure passes across the window.

"Mack?" Lew starts out of the dining room first, and Mistress and I track her into the hallway. Together, the three of us open the front door.

Something crouches on the porch behind the swing. It isn't Mack. The shoulders are too broad, the body too tall. This is a man.

Or something pretending to be a man.

It turns toward us, and a scream lodges halfway up my throat. The figure has no face. It's all shadows and confusion, and that forces Mistress and me back a step but not Lew. Lew's always been a fool. She steps to meet the darkness.

"Give her back," she says, and the thing without a mouth laughs.

I can do better than that. I can take you to her.

The darkness drifts toward her, and Lew lets out a guttural screech and pitches her skull at the place where its face should be. It catches her trinket midair and wraps its fingers around the temples. At once, the skull shatters into a thousand pieces, and though Lew's braver than Mack and raises her fist to the shadows, she can't get ahold of it like it can hold her.

One scream, and the shadows devour her.

Now there's another scream—my scream—as I fall to my knees and search the detritus for her. The shattered pieces of Lew's skull embed in my palms, and I drip red on the porch floor. I scream again and keep screaming, and I won't stop, my hands desperately trying to reassemble her. But she's part of the darkness now, and collecting these fragments won't put her back together.

"Rhee." Mistress's voice behind me is distant and strange. "Come on."

"Wait," I say, still fumbling with cracked bone, my fingers slick with my own blood. "Just let me try."

"You don't have time." Her hand is strong and cold on my shoulder, and that's when I look up and see what she sees. The darkness is moving after me and over me and trying to get into me.

This isn't like the last time with Mack. The darkness isn't satisfied with merely stealing Lew. He wants us too. Shadows drip toward us like tar, and we stumble back inside and shove the front door closed behind us. But that's what he wants. He wants us in one place where there's nowhere left to hide.

Mistress and I edge backward into the dining room as the hurricane lamps flicker before extinguishing altogether. Though it's almost too dark to see, there's enough light for us to glimpse what happens next. The ceiling sags overhead, and bits of pale tile fall on us. The smaller fragments are like snow on our eyelashes, but the larger, jagged pieces gouge our shoulders and neck. We yelp and pluck them out and press ourselves into the corners, but the whole room quivers and turns against us. The wallpaper peels off the plaster like stiff flesh in a taxidermist's hands. Everything in the house is alive and determined. Red screams my name as the mirror shakes and shifts on its nail, and she falls. I dive after her and catch her before she hits the floor, before she shatters into nothing. Undeterred, the wallpaper curls toward us, nipping at my feet and ankles and thighs. I crawl away on my back, kicking and flailing and pulling the mirror with me. In the doorway, Mistress yanks me up, and we run toward the hall. I cradle Red against me, my palms leaving red handprints on the glass.

Outside, darkness drapes over the house, our own burial shroud. I gaze through all the windows and the cracks in the door, but there's no world left out there. No front porch. No garden. Nothing beyond these walls and this moment. He's sealed us inside the house.

And this time, we're not leaving until he's finished with us.

chapter seven

MISTRESS GRABS MY HAND, AND WE CLAMBER FOR THE STAIRS. BUT THE darkness is there before us, dripping down each step, and that figure from the porch forms again in front of our eyes, stronger and more defined than before.

Now it has a face with two dark eyes smiling at me. I turn away to keep myself from screaming.

"Come on." Mistress yanks me toward the basement.

I bite down on air and brace against her. There couldn't be a worse place for us to hide. One way in—down the splintered steps with no backs—and no other way out. It's the only room in the house I've avoided for years. It was Mack's domain, and that gave me an excuse to eschew it, but that wasn't the real reason I avoided it. I couldn't stand it because I felt trapped there. Mack didn't need to build a coffin down there—the whole place was a sepulcher already.

But now, we have no choice. With the darkness pouring into all the cracks and filling up the rooms, we've got nowhere else.

We dash for the basement and lock the door behind us.

After a long moment, something knocks on the other side.

I stuff my fingers in my mouth and press myself against the door, but it thrusts its weight against me. Mistress sprints down the stairs and tosses Mack's leftover boards up to me. I barricade the door, shoving the lumber beneath the knob to keep it from turning. A fool's move, but one that holds for the moment. And all we have are these moments, fleeting and cruel as they are.

I creep down the stairs to Mistress, both of us breathless in the dark.

"Can you get us out?" she whispers.

I hold the mirror tighter. "Maybe."

I close my eyes and try to focus, try to see anything except this place, but the shadows are everywhere. They're all around me and in me, too, pulsing through my body like poison. They want us here.

I try again. I strain through the darkness and the rank tastes of fear and blood and oblivion to see past this moment. To see David and the highway and those crumbling potholes that I memorized a lifetime ago. But in my mind, it's all empty spaces where my memories should be. I choke back a sob. Once upon a time, the darkness stole my life from me. Now it's stealing my hereafter too.

I shake my head. "I'm sorry," I say, every muscle in my body limp and paralyzed.

A single bulb dangles overhead, turning our skin a jaundiced yellow.

This is it. This is where we go to die.

No, that's not right. Mistress, Red, and I have died once already. We're practically pros at that. This will be worse. We'll be less than nothing, no better than white noise buried behind the woodwork. How can anything be less than what we already are?

I lean back against the wall, desperate to catch my breath. The basement is filled with the light sweetness of carnations. Mack's scent. She should be here. This is where she belongs.

Now only an echo of her remains. Down here in the damp and the cold, you can still hear her, those soft weeps, the cries of an abandoned child.

And there's someone else here too. Another weeping girl in the walls. But these sobs are different. They brim with rage the color of late autumn when all the trees have blistered to orange ruins and blackened bark. A fury that wanes more with every passing moment because the darkness pulls her farther from us.

Lew.

Mistress crawls halfway up the wall, her vines the shape of spider legs, her dying foliage as sticky and pale as webbing.

"Lew? Mack? Where are you?" Her voice is urgent, every word tumbling over the next, blurring together with the cadence of a drunken man. "Tell us, please, tell us, and we'll come to you. I promise. We'll come for you."

But there's no reply. Not that we should be foolish enough to expect one.

Mistress collapses on the stone floor, her hands veiling her face. "I'm so sorry," she says, and I'm not sure if she's talking to Lew or to me or to herself. I just watch as she rocks back and forth like a censured child, the weight of regret heavy on her body. It's heavy on all of us, what we should have said and done and not taken for granted. The family we had together—and squandered.

But they're not the only family we've lost. From far away, the twins' voices rattle through the walls. They shouldn't be able to reach us here, but everything is permeable and unraveling.

"Rhee? Red? Where are you?"

"Can you hear them?" Red whispers to me, and I grip her tighter as we listen.

"We found something," the twins say. "Where are you? We need to show you."

But we'll never know what it is. I focus on their voices and pull myself toward them, pull all of us toward them. But the darkness presses against me, and I feel it in my bones, so aching and heavy, that I can't push past it. I can't escape.

There are others here too. Gladys calls out, her voice quaking and mournful. "Lew, darling, where are you? I can't see you, Lew. Talk to me."

And David rings through for a moment as well, only he isn't speaking to me.

"It's not what you think," he says. "Or who you think."

His wife. He must be talking to his wife. I shouldn't hear this, and I don't even want to, but our world is bleeding into theirs, everything overlapping because we've gone to them so many times and now we've brought them to us.

And if only we could get back to them. But it's too late for that.

Overhead, the bare bulb flickers and snuffs out altogether. The last light in the house is now gone.

Are you ready, pretty ones? Because I'm ready for you.

It appears first in the corner, curtaining toward us like billows of black silk. I rush to Mistress, my hands fumbling to pull her away, but she shoves me back, just as the darkness grasps her around the waist and uses her bloodroot and foxglove to wrap her up tight, her own body becoming a sarcophagus.

Still free, the wayward vine—my old enemy—whips at the shadows, this way and that, frantic to save Mistress, but it's not enough. With ethereal fingers, the darkness grips the green scamp and yanks hard, so hard that something cracks like bone. When he unclenches his hand, the vine has been severed in two, reduced to a crumble of cinders.

I edge backward against the wall, not wanting to flee, to be so craven as to leave Mistress behind. But she looks at me, her eyes swirling black, her skin like dried brush about to ignite.

"Run," she whispers, her last word before the gloom envelops her and she dissolves into nothing.

For once, I do as Mistress says. I mount the steps, Red clutched against me, her breath as ragged as mine. If we're meant to die here in this house, then we won't just wait for it. We'll choose the place it happens.

And we won't hide. Not now. Not ever again.

We're up the stairs and out into the hallway. I swing open the front door, and the darkness meets us there.

Not so fast, pretty. I'm not done with you yet.

With a flick of an invisible wrist, the shadows knock me back, and I cling to Red as I hit the wall and topple to the floor. We crawl backward into the dining room, and I pull myself to the cabinet in the corner filled with Lew's stash of booze. The darkness creeps closer, and I pitch the dust-caked bottles of mead and brandy and high-proof rum at the shadows, the thick glass shattering against the peeled wallpaper and flaccid velvet curtains. When those are all gone, I scamper to the sideboard and toss every hurricane lamp, dousing the decor with the sour stench of kerosene.

The darkness chortles, and it ricochets off all the corners of the room. *You can't hurt me, pretty Mary. Nothing can.*

My chest constricts because I know he's right. He'll outlast us. He'll keep going. It will never end. He'll never stop, not until he's captured every one of us.

I glare into him, my hatred burning bright inside me. But if he's going to take everything of mine, I can at least take something of his first. This house was furnished when we got here. It was ready for us. And I can do the next occupants a favor. I can make sure that there's nothing left.

David's matchbook flashes up from the floor. If he's sliding in and out, solid and not solid, maybe this souvenir is the same way. Maybe I can hold it in my hand.

My jaw clenched, I focus on the blue paperboard, and like the reflection in the mirror, I change it. But instead of turning it liquid like the glass, I make it real and whole. All my lingering fear melts away, and I tear off one flimsy stick. If this ends tonight, let this be my last choice. And perhaps my best one.

I strike the match and drop it where I stand. The flames crawl across the floor and blossom up the walls and curtains. In an instant, the whole room is alight. It's warm and bright and glorious.

The darkness grimaces and charges at us, but the fire estranges us from him, and he can't breach the blaze. We're inside a ring of flames, and he can't touch us. This is better. This is so much better than I expected.

But that doesn't mean we're safe. The fire turns the tips of my hair black, and embers dance to the floor.

"Rhee," Red says, the mirror heating up and turning liquid around the edges. "What do we do?"

My skin seethes on my bones, and handfuls of me drip to the floor like colorless cake batter. This is it. One last try. I close my eyes.

David. The highway. That place I've hated and dreaded and wanted to be free of forever.

I see it in my mind. And I start pulling myself toward it. I pull Red and me toward somewhere outside this moment. The darkness towers over us, desperate to reach through the flames with his long fingers, but I won't look at him. I won't see the face he's invented for himself, a masquerade to pretend he's something close to human.

The house shudders around us, its fiery death throes, and I know it's almost too late. The walls tumble down, and the fire reaches my marrow, but I hold onto the image of the highway. I hold it tight. I won't let the memory of who I was—who I *am*—slip away this time. The mirror cradled in my arms, I fall backward into somewhere else, leaving the house for the last time with the darkness behind me still calling my name.

chapter eight

WE FLOAT THROUGH THE HERE AND THERE, OUR BODIES SUSPENDED IN nothing. I don't know where we'll end up, and I don't care. At least we're out of that house. For good this time.

And then we're on the highway. Right where I belong. But not quite. There's a sharp glare blinding me, and beneath us, the concrete shimmers with heat. I've never seen it like this.

In the daylight.

"We're on the wrong side of night," Red murmurs inside the mirror, and she's right. And the sunshine must act the same as the fire because the darkness isn't here, whispering in my ear, his long fingers tugging at me.

The mirror gripped in my shaking hands, I linger for a moment, exposed in the open. My body is scorched and tired and heavy from the fire. If I were still human, I'd be dead. But I'm not human, not anymore, so I'm fine. Or as close to fine as I can get.

Inside the reflection, two candy-sweet voices whisper. "Bloody Mary."

Red turns to me. "The twins are calling," she says.

On the shoulder of the road, I nestle the mirror in the underbrush, keeping it safe from anyone who might find it here. I'm not even sure if it's visible. I'm not sure if I'm visible in the daylight either.

"Bloody Mary," the twins repeat.

I reach through the reflection, and with a steady hand, Red guides me in. I try to pull her out instead, try to free her to be with me, but she just shakes her head, and I slip inside.

"Bloody Mary," they say and materialize through the reflection. It's the middle of the day, but the two of them are still in those ratty wedding gowns, their veils curled over their faces, the curtains in their bedrooms drawn to enhance the flickering of their ivory taper candles.

They glare at us in mock anger. "We've been calling you all night. Where have you two been?"

Nowhere good, I want to say. But I ask something else. "Are you okay? I mean—" I hesitate. "Have you experienced any side effects from your visit the other night?"

Like David. Have they become like David?

The twins brighten. "Oh, that." They stick their whole hands through the burning wax and giggle. "Cool, right?"

Red chokes on air. "No, not cool," she says, her lips peeled back in a stern line, looking very much like an angry big sister. "Vanishing like a ghost is not cool. It's bad, okay?"

The twins shrug. "If you say so." They edge closer to the mirror, their breath fogging up the glass. "Do you want to hear about what we found?"

"Yes," I say.

"We know where you belong, Rhee. Or at least where you're from."

The mirror turns liquid, and they give me a folded piece of pink bubblegum-scented paper. I shouldn't be able to touch it, but I can. Scribbled in block letters is an address.

"The place is at the end of the highway you haunt," they say. "At the county line near the airport."

I grip the note tightly between my fingers. This might be for nothing. I'm not sure if I can even move past the same stretch I've always taken on the highway.

Red squeezes my arm, her hand warm and smelling of cinnamon and rose. "You'll get there," she whispers. "You'll figure out a way."

The twins stare back at us, their complexions pale yellow in the fading glow of candlelight. "Will you come back to us tonight?"

"If we can," Red says.

The twins nod as though this answer will have to do. They bow their heads, and their reflections fade away.

Inside the darkened mirror, Red and I are alone, and it feels strange to know there's only us now. No home. No family. Maybe no future past this moment.

"We'll wait for dark," I say, still gripping the slip of paper. "Then we'll go to this place."

Red shakes her head and starts to say something, but from far off, a voice comes for us—for her—and this time, it's not the twins. This sound is all razorblades and poison apples.

"Bloody Mary." The words drape over us like a funerary shroud, and everything fades to a sullen gray. My body seizes up. There is no daylight here, nothing to keep the darkness out. He can reach inside the mirror if he wants. He can pluck us from this place like the last petal off a wilted corsage.

Red gazes at me, her face bright and clear and brave. "It's my turn now," she says. "That leaves you, Rhee."

"Me?" My eyes blur with salt and sorrow. "What am I supposed to do?"

The walls rumble around us as if the whole world is laughing.

"Bloody Mary." The sing-song burns through me. It's nearer now, a hot breath on my cheek.

Red's hand grasps mine, and she steadies my quivering. "You need to leave now." Her voice is burning and urgent and pressing into the sagging cage of my bones. "You can stop him, Rhee. I know you can."

I shake my head, and the tears come harder now. Tears I didn't even know I could cry. "I won't leave you."

"You don't get to choose that," she says. "I get to choose."

The glass turns liquid, and from every direction, the voice speaks into us. "Bloody Mary."

And we're suddenly not alone. The darkness with its wide shoulders and ugly visage gawks at us through the mirror. It steps inside, joining us like a giddy schoolboy around a Ouija board.

In this moment, the last moment, Red looks at me, her fingers still entwined with mine, and I sense it in her face before I feel it. I'm dissolving. I'm leaving this place. She's doing this to me. With all the strength left in her, she sends me away into the here and there. Far from her and what's come to claim her.

I fall backward from her, and the last thing I see before I vanish is the darkness enfold her like velvet at midnight. The sinews that bind us together snap, and everything in me turns inside out, shredded and torn and destroyed.

Before I can yell out, I'm on the highway, nauseous and disoriented. I collapse to my knees next to the mirror, sinking into the concrete, my bones slipping past the asphalt and potholes.

The shadow laughs from inside the empty reflection, too craven to show himself in the light.

I choke down salt and snot. "Don't do this," I say. "Not this time. Not to her." *It's already done.*

The mirror shatters in my hands. Shards jab into my wrists and palms and fingertips, the blood warm and dark as mulled wine. For an instant, she's there, all the broken pieces of Red. She parts her lips to scream, but she's ripped away and melted from existence. And when it's over, the pieces of the mirror are only glass, see-through and useless. There's no more reflection.

He's stolen everything she was.

Red might not be able to scream, but I can. My head lolls back, and I exhale a banshee wail that chases all the crows from the trees. The pain unfurls from me like black lace on a spool, like something yanked hard that unravels before you have a chance to stop it. Everything pours out of me, and I don't stop until my throat is hoarse and my body too weak to fight or cry or move again.

I curl in the dirt for what feels like a lifetime. I don't want to leave this place. I don't want to go to the address the twins gave me. I just want to wait for the end. But an engine cuts out next to me, and someone's here to change my mind. Someone in a dinged-up station wagon.

"You're early," I wheeze.

David creeps closer, staring at me as if he's not sure I'm real. He apparently believes in ghosts, just not ghosts in daylight.

"I heard you," he says at last. "From across town, I heard you screaming. It was like a thousand bubbles bursting in my blood."

That's how it felt for me too.

He sucks in a heavy breath. "And your sisters? Are they—"

"Gone," I say, and he nods as though he'd already guessed.

In the backseat, Abby murmurs in her sleep, her dreams fitful and faraway.

I gaze at her through the window. "She shouldn't be here."

David grunts. "And where would she be safer?"

"With your wife," I say, but he shakes his head.

"She's gone," he says. "Said it's her turn now to have some space. She left Abby with me, and I'm not leaving her with anyone else."

I look hard at him. "And if you fade out like a ghost? If you just vanish?"

"Then at least she'll be here, so I can say goodbye."

I show him the address on the piece of paper the twins gave me, and we start there. At first, I'm convinced David will have to go without me and return with his best recap, but the car breezes past the cemetery fence, and I keep going, here in the passenger's seat. This is daylight now. Everything is different. I'm not held in by invisible borders.

But I'm the only one who's still free. All the way along the highway, I can hear my family. From somewhere far beyond this road, Mistress weeps as do Lew and Mack. Red isn't like them. She doesn't just sob. She also calls my name, her wails mournful and thin. My skin buzzes because I can't help her, not right now, not from here. All I can do is cover my mouth with both hands and try not to scream.

"Are you okay?" David watches me.

"Hurry," I whisper. "Please hurry."

We arrive half an hour before sunset. When it comes into view, I nearly choke on the sight. This isn't what I wanted. It's no beautiful dancehall where I had my last waltz or a lovely family estate passed down through generations. It's less than a house, a simple shack, abandoned and forgotten, the cheap white veneer peeling off the siding as though even the paint wants to escape it.

I climb out of the car and stare at it. This is everything I've dreaded. David doesn't say anything at first. With an unsteady hand like he can't trust his own body, he lifts a still sleeping Abby from her car seat and carries her behind me.

"Do you remember this place?" he asks at last.

I heave in, sniffling. "I hope not."

A plane passes over us, and the engines rumble deep inside me, familiar and lonely. I hold my breath as we open the front door.

The inside is even worse. No art deco design, no vaulted ceilings. It's a plain, square space, nowhere near as decadent and elegant as the expansive third floor I used to occupy. I creep into the living room. The picture window is cracked, the spider web just as I remembered it.

David tracks behind me, and I just shake my head, because this can't be it. This can't be my home.

In the sallow light of late afternoon, we turn down a narrow hallway and find a tiny bedroom at the end of the corridor. David opens the door, and the stale scents of motor oil and orange peel overwhelm us. Ragged curtains hang from all the windows. At first, I think the fabric is gray until I step closer and see it. A faded blue and white gingham.

"Rhee?" David watches me, but I'm looking at something else.

A cobweb-caked Victrola sits sullenly in the corner next to a pile of Glenn Miller and Louis Armstrong and Bennie Goodman, their faces fanned out and faded with sun and years.

These records are mine. This place is mine.

My knees weaken, and a whole lifetime passes through me in an instant.

I remember everything. The loneliness, the nothing life I spent alone in this room, turning records and waiting for life to start. It never did, not for me.

And now I wonder if forgetting might have been better.

"So," David says, his voice shaking, "who were you?"

I heave out a rueful laugh. Inside, I'm empty, so painfully empty I almost can't speak.

"I was no one," I say, and it's true, oh god, it's true.

The girl from David's book was never me. She was the ghost who haunted me. The ghost I replaced.

My fingertips graze the walls, nearly feeling the residue of my life there. "The previous Resurrection Mary came to me because we were alike."

And that's it. That's who the Marys are. We're no one. The easy marks. The strange girls discarded by the world, the ones nobody would miss, our lives passed by and wasted. When the ghost who visited me was all used up like we are now, the darkness swapped me for her.

Her eyelids heavy, Abby slips from David's arms and climbs on the bed that used to be mine. The mattress is mildewed and stained, but she doesn't mind. She just bounces and squeals and smiles up at us.

A chill settles deep inside me. She can see me. She could see all of us, even once we were fading. That's because she's like us. She's someone the darkness will choose. Maybe that's his plan: to replace me with Abby, just like he'll replace Red with the twins. I can hear his scratchy, hideous voice now when he comes for the twins: *Two pretty Marys for the price of one.*

No. He won't steal them. That, I'll make sure of. He won't have any of them. My sisters aren't gone, not completely. Their weeping still haunts me. And even if their sobs are fading, they're still here, still reachable.

It's not too late.

Outside, the sun dips in the sky. The darkness is almost here.

I kneel next to the bed, next to Abby. "You rest now," I say. "But no matter what happens, you stay right here in this room. Do you understand?"

She blinks up at me, her clear brown eyes the color of mine. "I understand, Aunt Rhee."

She curls up to sleep, and David closes the door behind us.

Together, we linger in the moldering living room. This is my domain, just like the coffin was Mack's and the porch was Lew's and the mirror was Red's. This is where he will come for me.

But he won't get the chance. I'll go to him first. I'll head into the darkness—through the shadows of these walls and out of this place into the space between. I'll meet him there. No fear. No melancholy. Only me and him.

I steady my breath and tell David my plan. "Wait until it's nearly sunrise," I say. "Then follow me in and come for them."

My sisters. They'll be there, weeping in the dark. I know they will. And David will be able to reach them, now that our worlds are sliding together, and he's stuck in between, the same as me.

"And what about you?" he asks.

"I'll find my own way out." It's a lie, one that David sees through instantly. I won't come back. The darkness will make sure of it. It spoke to me first and saved me for last. I'm integral to all of this, and that's fine. So long as we can retrieve my sisters, then that's something. That's worth it.

"And what now?" David asks, his eyes heavy and gray.

I gaze at him. If this is the end, there's one last thing I want to try. Part of David is like us now, trapped in between. Maybe once I'm gone and his last tether to the liminal space is severed, he'll be okay again. Maybe it's only because I'm in one place, and he's in another, and the two realms are sliding together. But in this moment, our worlds aren't so far apart.

In the house, I could hold his matchbook in my hand. Now maybe I can hold him too.

I stretch out my arms for his. David hesitates before reaching back. We don't slip through each other, but we're not entirely solid either. It's like touching water, the way our skin ripples together. But after all these years, it's not just something. It's everything.

Music from an ethereal Victrola rises through the air. "Moonlight Serenade." My favorite Glenn Miller song.

We sway together, side by side, our soft arms entangled. This is the closest to a first dance we'll ever know, and that's okay. It's more than I ever thought we'd share.

When the song is over and the sun slips from the sky, I turn away from him and move toward the shadows, toward the place I've always belonged.

I look back once and smile at David. He smiles too.

Then I face the darkness and step into the wall.

chapter nine

THE INSIDE OF THE HOUSE UNFOLDS INTO ANOTHER WORLD. A VAST SILVER ballroom with a steel vaulted ceiling higher than the clouds and endless rows of fancy tables, shrouded in dark linens like corpses awaiting autopsy.

This is for me. The darkness has crafted this ballroom just for me.

Music plays somewhere far off, but that's not what thrums within me. A murky wind rustles through the room, singing a requiem, so soft and lonely it makes me want to cry.

"You may shed a tear," someone says, "if you'd like."

The voice is clear and familiar and simmering in my ears, a melody that's really here and not confined only to my mind. Something made concrete.

"Hello," I say, and the darkness appears in front of me, descending slowly, piece by piece, a gentleman climbing out of a carriage from the sky. He stands at full height, towering over me, and he looks real now. Real and handsome and wicked as heartache.

I grimace away from him, and he laughs.

"Don't you like my new face?" He smiles. "Perhaps you'd prefer this one."

His body shifts, and his features soften. I blink, and I'm staring at David. Or rather, a hideous imitation of David.

"Stop," I say.

"But I thought you liked him." The darkness stands across from me yet whispers in my ear. "You've certainly gazed lovingly at him enough times."

My jaw clenches. "Return to what you were."

"As you like," he says, and his visage reverts back to his own.

I swallow hard. "Why are we here?" I ask, my voice splitting in two. "What do you want from me?"

"Don't you know?" The darkness eddies around me, over and over like a dance, and I intuit what he's doing. He's manipulating the hourglass. Each time he circles me, we lose another piece of the night. Time is slipping away quicker here. He's stealing it from me, the same way he's stolen everything else. He wants time to run out, so when morning comes, I'll be here where he wants me, in the place where I'll belong to him.

"Where are they?" I say. "Where are my sisters?"

"Don't you see them, Rhee?" He ripples toward me. "Why, they're right here."

The gloom shifts around me, and every fiber in my body goes numb. He's disguised the room, and only now can I see through the fantasy, through the phony image of the ballroom. There are no tables and chairs and fancy linens. There are no accoutrements here at all. There are only girls. A thousand rows of girls, recumbent and still.

Some are in coffins, sealed up tight. Some are shrouded in dead flowers and veiled in pink chiffon. Some are laid bare and lonely, nothing except their broken skulls or broken mirrors to protect them from the cold and the dark.

The rustling sound whispers past me, and I realize it isn't wind. It's their weeping, hundreds upon hundreds of girls sobbing through heavy dreams, their cries muffled and ever-fading. All these Marys that came before.

I pull away from the darkness and race through the maze of girls, desperate to discover my sisters, to rouse them before it's too late. But these labyrinthine aisles stretch on forever, and the darkness is always faster than me.

He skips across the ceiling and materializes at my side. "Where ever are you going, pretty Rhee?"

"Give them back to me," I say, and it's a hopeless request, but I have to stall him, I have to find my sisters on my own. Then I can direct David to them when he comes at dawn. A dawn that is nearer now, so near I can nearly taste its buttery sweetness. David will come, and he'll salvage them. Somehow, he'll get them out of here.

I twist away and keep walking, down a long, dizzying row of girls, the darkness my constant companion. But then what of the other Marys? There are too many of them to rescue in one night. And how can we leave them here for the shadows to torment and possess?

But I can't think of the others now. I can't think of anything except my four sisters.

"I've watched you, Rhee," the darkness whispers, soft and sweet as a lover. "For a lifetime, I've seen you. How you scare. Like haunting is a work of art."

"I've learned from the best." I gaze hard at him. "From my sisters."

"They aren't your sisters." His voice bristles. "But of course, you'd call them that. The lot of you were always trouble."

Trouble. This pleases me. We were trouble because we were a family. Because we were stronger together. For all his vicious alchemy, the darkness couldn't predict that. And he couldn't stop it.

I break into a sprint, cutting past two coffins and a pile of brush that was once a girl like Mistress. These are close imitations but still imitations. Everything here is strained illusion.

The darkness meets me at the end of the corridor. I turn and try to run again, past a girl with mirror glass embedded in her skin—a previous Red, though not my Red—but the darkness cuts me off. He's everywhere, and I can't escape him.

"The others weren't like you." He flashes me a smile that looks more like a sneer. "They grew weaker, but you became stronger. That's because you're like me. There's always been darkness in you."

I stop in the center of the room, the still point of a hurricane. "That's a lie."

He grins, a real grin this time. "No, it's not," he says, and he's right. I hate it, but he's right. I've always relished a good scare. It's never bothered me, never haunted me like it should have. I've been better in death than I ever was in life.

"And what will happen to all of them?" I motion to the girls, the disorienting rows repeating to infinity.

The darkness leans in close, and I taste his breath, all jagged ice and coffin dirt and winters that never end. "They're slumbering well enough," he says. "You wouldn't want to disturb them. That would be rude, don't you think?"

"Not as rude as stealing a girl's afterlife."

He scoffs, and the dust in all the shadows shudders in refrain. "You had your chance at life, and you wasted it. I plucked you from nothing, from less than obscurity. And I transformed you into a legend."

"A fleeting legend," I say. "You use us up until we're no good. Until there's nothing left of us."

"Not me." He smiles. "The world is the one that uses you up. People forget the stories after a while. The new ghosts are bright and eager and make them remember again."

My fingers curl into talons. "And there'll always be more girls, ripe and ready for the taking, isn't that right?" I ask, and he shrugs. That's how he sees it, as a daisy chain of ghosts. The twins and Abby and all those who could see us, who embraced us, will become just like us. We've condemned them without ever meaning to.

"But you're not like the others," he says and grasps my hand in his. "I don't want to put you away with them. I want you to stay with me."

I know what this means. I have to pick between two impossible existences: either he devours me tonight, the same as he devoured the others, or he spends an eternity devouring me in another way.

And I have to choose. Right now.

"I'll stay," I say and step to meet him. "On one condition."

He smirks. "What's that?"

"First, you dance with me."

He hesitates, convinced it's a trick. But when he can divine no angle, he reaches forth and takes my other hand, and amidst ethereal music of my own making, we waltz. It's not sweet, like with David, but coarse and regimented, every step aching in its precision. And he doesn't try to hide what he's doing. With one palm pressed into my back and the other shackled around my wrist, he's drawing me in, closer to him, until there's no way to tell where he ends and I begin. This is what he wants. I'm fading, the darkness siphoning me away, slowly, as though I won't notice. He's weakening me, making me pliable and translucent and nothing at all. Easier to control. Easier to call his own. And I let him. I let him because it's almost time. It's almost dawn.

David sneaks in through the wall, through the path I left open for him, and with my focus razor-sharp, I shroud him and the entrance in darkness, blotting out the barrier between here and there. I still don't know where my sisters are, but maybe David will find them in time.

I twirl in a waltz, a Glenn Miller song surging over the weeps of the Marys, the music hiding David's footsteps as he creeps down the rows.

I hold the darkness closer to me, but even as I guide him away from David, he senses it. My trickery.

The darkness whirls me around until I'm dazed and weak before he yanks me down an avenue of girls. For an instant, I see them—my sisters. And David next to them, desperately trying to awaken them.

Without shifting from my side, the darkness lifts David from his feet, those long fingers wrapped around his throat, even at a distance. "And what shall we do about him?"

"Don't," I whisper, though my voice is lost in the waning music and waning sobs.

"We could always scare him into oblivion," the darkness says as David squirms midair. "And of course, we could make his devilish little progeny one of our own."

I steel my body against the shadows. "Leave them alone," I say.

The darkness smiles. "Or what?"

I gaze into his face, into that terrible face, and something ignites inside me. A tiny flicker that burns so bright I can hardly bear it. My own gloom. It's what's always been there. It's what made the darkness want me, and though he's drained so much of it away, I'm still me. With every shred of power left in me, I reach out, my own hands invisible, and release the shroud that hides the barrier between here and there. On the other side, back in the shack that was once my home, morning has broken, and the light pours in through the cracked picture window. In an instant, it breaches this faux ballroom and sears through us.

In my arms, the darkness screams—a darkness that can't be joined with fire or light—and I feel it. The fear in him. Until this moment, I wasn't sure, but now I know: even the wickedest things can feel fear. It unfurls from deep within him, and his body burns up until all that remains of him is smoke and dread.

Smiling, I inhale and devour him whole.

Panting, David falls to the floor at my feet, and I linger here among these rows of sleeping girls.

Maybe this is over. Maybe we won.

But then something new shifts within me. My skins boils on my flesh, and I know I'm wrong. This isn't what I wanted. The darkness, all cold and candy-sweet, is within me now, a part of me like I was once part of him. He crawls inside me, a spider up a sleeve, and with my body fading away after what he's done to me, there's almost nothing left. I'm more shadow now than I am me. And with him coursing inside my veins and merging with my own darkness, I can guess what comes next. I'll become the new emissary, the one to gather together the girls. The captor, boundless and cruel. Everything is a cycle, and I'll be the newest part of it.

No. I'd rather become nothing at all. I'd rather fade away right here.

My gloom dwindling into his, I part my lips and wail. This is enough to reach my sisters. Without him to chain them down, my pain awakens them from their cruel dreams.

With a steady hand, Mack lifts open her coffin, and Lew cobbles together her skull before rising to her feet. Never one to be outdone, Mistress shifts from the ash that used to be her garden, and she drifts toward me, more fearsome than before. They gather together around me, my family united one last time.

David is here too. He kneels over me, searching the air helplessly. "I can't see her." His words are strangled and wet. "Rhee? Where is she? I can't see her."

"She's here," Mack says, but the quiver in her voice belies the truth: the other Marys can barely see me themselves. I'm fading before their eyes. They huddle together, frantic to find me and anchor me here. Lew leans against Mack, and Mack grips the hand of someone else. Someone I hardly recognize outside of the obscure gray of the mirror.

Red. Here she is, out in the open, whole and real and unconfined. It's like I'm seeing her for the first time.

"You're beautiful." I reach for her hand, but I slip right through her. She smiles at what's left of me and bites back her tears.

"We need to do something," Mistress says, proper and resolute as always. At her feet, something sinuous and determined whips through me. The vine. It's smaller now, down to the nub where the darkness tore it in two, but it flicks at me, trying to coax me back. They're all trying to coax me back, my four sisters and David too. But even together, they're not enough to ground me here. I'm slipping away.

Perhaps this is for the best. The darkness will end with me. I close my eyes and wait for my body to dim beneath the shadows. But my rest is not to be.

"Why are all these pretty ghosts sleeping?" A tiny voice like a cathedral bell at midnight rings through the ballroom. "And where's Aunt Rhee? I heard her crying."

Abby. I told her to stay out of here, but she didn't listen to me. Of course, she didn't. A chance to meet the beyond? I wouldn't have listened to me either.

A shadow passes across my face, and I open my eyes. Abby looms over me and grins.

"It's okay, Daddy," she says. "I've found her."

"You can see her?" David waves his hands uselessly in the air as if I'm deliberately hiding there. "Baby, you see her?"

"Sure, she's right here." Abby wraps her chubby fingers around mine, and in this moment, I'm not a ghost at all. I'm only a girl, real and whole.

This is all wrong. She shouldn't be able to touch me. But then she shouldn't have ever been destined to become my replacement either. That fate binds us together. We're the same and not the same. I'm the end she never suffered, and she's the beginning I never got. And with her at my side, I can feel it stirring within me. The darkness thrashes, but it can't bubble to the surface. If it tries, Abby will simply grin and chase it away.

"Are you feeling all right, Aunt Rhee?" Abby dabs the sweat and grime from my forehead. "You look tired today."

I rasp out a laugh. "I am tired, little one. So very tired."

"Let's get out of here." Abby glances around, her nose scrunched up. "It's not very nice in this place."

She tugs my hand and leads me out of the shadows and through the wall. David and my sisters follow us, each of them murmuring my name. They can no longer see me, but that's okay. Abby guides me back to the dusty place that was my home all those years ago, back when I was alive. The home that I've found all over again.

Daylight, pure and unforgiving, pours across the stained floor, and the dust lilts through the air, gray and beautiful and free.

Through the cracked front window, I smile and look into the sun.

chapter ten

"AUNT RHEE, WOULD YOU LIKE TO PLAY HIDE-AND-SEEK?"

Abby blinks up at me, wide-eyed and pleading, and I chuckle because she knows I won't deny her.

"Yes, baby," I say, "I would love to."

She leads me outside to the biggest oak tree, the one that towers over the sagging roof of the house. The sap once again drips from the branches, clear and sweet as rainwater. It's spring and warm and welcoming. In the backyard, I extend my arms over my head and chase Abby across the overgrown grass. She squeals and runs off, eager to pick a hiding place where even a ghost can't find her.

I cover my eyes and start counting. The sun shines down and prickles my skin. Unlike the darkness that came before me, I don't turn to ash in the day. I'm not pure gloom and never have been—my sisters and David and Abby make sure of that.

The morning smells sweet and fresh, and the bottoms of my feet itch, ready to rise up to meet the clouds. And I could float away if I wanted to. No longer tethered to earth, I could float anywhere in the world now. But why would I? If I drifted away, I would spoil one little girl's perfect game of hide-and-seek. And that would be an unforgivable offense.

After I call out a hundred, I creep around the yard and back into the house. In the corner of the living room, David toils away at decades' worth of repairs. This home, decrepit as it is, isn't only mine anymore. Over the winter, David paid off the long-simmering lien and purchased the property—for a decent bargain since none of the locals were hankering for a haunted house with bad pipes. Now he's fixing it up the way it used to be, the way I remember it. I whisper to Abby all the little details—the gingham curtains in the bedroom and the robin egg blue paint for the walls—and she sprawls out on the floor, her lips twisted to one side as she employs a kaleidoscope of Crayolas to craft her best likeness. I can't quite describe it like I see it in my mind, and Abby can't quite draw it the way I describe, so the finished home won't be perfect. But then nothing ever is.

"It's a fresh start," David told his wife, though it didn't quite convince her. She hasn't moved in, not yet, but she visits often and watches the repairs and sees David, the same way I see him, kind and flawed and human. Their future is a fragile one, but that's better than no future at all.

My future is fragile too. Except for flashes here and there, David still can't see me. No one but Abby can. And the darkness isn't gone. In quiet moments, I hear him whispering to me, tugging at me, desperate to claw his way out. But I won't let him. I won't listen. There might always be shadow, but there will be light too. And sometimes, that's enough.

Abby peeks out of her hiding place in the hallway and grins at me. I smile back at her.

Yes, this time, the light will be enough.

Though they can't see me either, my sisters return here often, paying their respects. And their disrespects.

"This place is a mess." Mistress drags one manicured finger across a grimy cornice, her body more substantial than before. My sisters are still ghosts, but they're a little more alive too. They can touch this world and live in it. David can live in it too. He no longer flashes in and out like a phantom. Neither do the twins. With the darkness tethered, no longer able to yank us back and forth, we're stable here. Or as stable as a world filled with spirits can ever be.

The afternoon light slants golden through the front window, and the spider-web crack in the glass casts lines on all my sisters' faces. Here we are, the way we're meant to be: a family of ghosts, five Marys in one place, with Abby in the middle as my decoder.

"Aunt Rhee says she's glad to see you," Abby says, nodding once, proud of herself.

They give me their updates like old folks back from a chartered tour of the Taj Mahal. Mack has found a nice funeral home to haunt in Cleveland, and Mistress has been touring all the gardens on earth, from California to Moscow.

"You wouldn't believe all the poisonous plants I'd never even heard of!" she marvels.

Red hides among the stacks of withered textbooks in the twins' house, the three of them researching the Marys, remembering who we are, cataloging us for posterity, and of course, terrorizing the twins' parents whenever they come home for a visit.

"Sometimes," Red says, leaning toward me, toward the place she thinks I am, "we materialize in the bathroom mirror. You know, for old time's sake."

For her part, Lew's retired to Des Moines where Gladys is teaching her all the trade secrets of a self-respecting blue-haired lady. Bingo games and knitting circles and, of course, baking tips.

"If I focus hard enough, I can even hold a wooden spoon now!" Lew beams and shares Gladys's snickerdoodle recipe, which she claims makes the "best cookies this side of the Mississippi."

Her eyes burning bright, Abby listens to cheerful tales of desserts she's never sampled. "Aunt Rhee doesn't believe you," Abby says. "You should bring some cookies with you next time to prove it."

I laugh and shake my head. I never said that. But I won't ruin Abby's caper.

"I'll see what I can do, little one," Lew says, flashing her a grin.

Sunset grows nearer, and my sisters bid their farewells.

"Those mortals won't terrify themselves," Mistress says.

I smile and wave a goodbye none of them can see, always a little lonely inside that their visits end too soon.

Red lingers behind, hopeful she might catch a glimpse of me. But no matter how many times we circle each other, I can't bring myself into her focus. Now I'm a ghost in a way I never was before.

With a defeated sigh, she turns away.

"Goodbye," I say, my fingers gliding through her hair. That long mane is no longer caked thick with blood. Now it's shining and wild and hers.

At my touch, Red starts for a moment, a shiver trembling through her. She smiles.

"I'll see you soon, Rhee," she says, and I hope she's right.

After my sisters have departed and the sun evaporates from the sky, David mops the sweat from his forehead and closes up his toolbox. Another day has escaped us. Somehow, I thought a life would pass slower if I could live it one sunrise at a time, but each one is gone before I even have a chance to hold it in my hand.

In my old room, I sit by David's side as he reads Abby a bedtime story about a wolf and a girl draped in red. Curled up in her new bed, Abby chortles and requests an encore when the tale is over, but she falls asleep before the little girl fills the beast's belly with stone. It's probably for the best. I don't think those stones would work anyhow. Fire would have been better. Trust me on that.

Down the hall, David kicks off his boots and climbs into his own bed. I sit on the edge of the mattress, my hands folded in my lap, and he turns and smiles at me, at the air I occupy.

"Goodnight, Rhee," he says and dims the light. I recline next to him, his breathing calm in the dark. I want to linger here, tucked against him as he dozes off, our bodies so close we might as well be one.

But I can't stay. My work has waited long enough. Before I slip out the door, I kiss David's forehead, my lips as ephemeral as air, never disturbing his sleep.

Through the wall, the Marys are sleeping too, thousands of them murmuring in their strange dreams. Together in their neat rows, they no longer weep, but that doesn't mean they're at peace. This still isn't their choice. Some of them have merely been asleep so long they no longer remember how to open their eyes. But I'm here now, and I'll help them.

I march down the rows of girls whose faces I've memorized. There are so many of them, their bodies dusty and quiet, and sometimes it feels overwhelming, as though this should never be the work of a single person. But then I smile and remember: I have an eternity to rouse them from this place. And that's what I'll do. One by one, I'll retrieve them from the darkness, and the legends will be free, the way they were meant to be. Then maybe I'll be free too.

And tonight, I know where to start. Far off in the corner beneath a gauzy spotlight where the Glenn Miller music plays on repeat, I find her.

The Mary who came before me.

As the hours fade away until dawn, I sit with her and tell her everything. About all the secrets we shared and how beautifully terrifying she was, her hauntings a formidable sight. And I tell her that this was never her fault, that she deserves better, that she *is* better.

She's fabled. She's remembered. She matters.

This work is imperfect. There is no easy way to coax a spirit back. But I don't give up. I keep reminding her of herself, and somehow, she hears me. Still dozing, she wades through the darkness in this make-believe ballroom and through the darkness stirring deep within my bones. Her dreams aren't so distant and bottomless anymore. Her dreams aren't anything at all, fragments of the past, a cruel fate in need of sloughing off.

Her lips curl into a smile and so do mine.

"Awaken," I whisper, and the ghost opens her eyes.

§

Gwendolyn Kiste is a speculative fiction author based in Pennsylvania. Her short stories have appeared in *Nightmare, Shimmer, Interzone, Black Static,* and *Three-Lobed Burning Eye,* among other outlets. Her debut fiction collection, *And Her Smile Will Untether the Universe,* is available now from JournalStone.

A native of Ohio, she currently dwells on an abandoned horse farm outside of Pittsburgh with her husband, two cats, and not nearly enough ghosts. You can find her online at gwendolynkiste.com.

BROKEN EYE BOOKS

NOVELLAS
Izanami's Choice, by Adam Heine
Never Now Always, by Desirina Boskovich
Pretty Marys All in a Row, by Gwendolyn Kiste

NOVELS
The Hole Behind Midnight, by Clinton J. Boomer
Crooked, by Richard Pett
Scourge of the Realm, by Erik Scott de Bie

COLLECTIONS
Royden Poole's Field Guide to the 25th Hour, by Clinton J. Boomer

ANTHOLOGIES
(edited by Scott Gable & C. Dombrowski)
By Faerie Light: Tales of the Fair Folk
Ghost in the Cogs: Steam-Powered Ghost Stories
Tomorrow's Cthulhu: Stories at the Dawn of Posthumanity
Ride the Star Wind: Cthulhu, Space Opera, and the Cosmic Weird

Stay weird.
Read books.
Repeat.

brokeneyebooks.com

twitter.com/brokeneyebooks
facebook.com/brokeneyebooks